TRAP 4 LYFE: DOWN TO RIDE FOR A COMPTON MENACE

By: Bri Deshai

PROLOGUE

Money

"You ready to do this, bae?"

Kash pulled her mask over her face and nodded her head. Not being able to resist, I pulled her towards me and kissed her lips. There is nothing sexier than seeing my wife taking the life of a nigga who crossed us.

"Let's do this shit then." We both cocked our guns and broke into the back door. The eerie feeling of being watched came over me which instantly made me watch my surroundings. This is not the first time my wife and I had to handle our own business because my team wasn't able to, but every now and then we had to get our hands dirty. I felt around the wall to figure out where the light switch was since we were literally standing in darkness, and the first thing that I saw were two bitches standing in front of me with a shotgun.

"These bitches think they're tuff, huh daddy?" Kash mocked, handing me her gun.

"Who are you and what are you doing in this house?" One of them asked, trying to sound hard but was scared shitless.

"I don't like having conversations, little girl. Where is Gritt's grimy ass at?" I asked, walking closer to them.

"You got five seconds to get out of here before the both of you lose y'all life." Kash looked at me then burst out laughing.

"They thought that little threat was going to work on us, baby. You see, I was going to let y'all bitches live, but since both of you are talking out the side of y'all neck, I have to kill y'all." She handed me her gun and walked towards both of them not caring that they had guns in their hands. In one quick motion, Kash grabbed both of them and snapped their necks at the same time, making my dick hard.

"Damn baby, it turns me on when you get all gangsta on me," I whispered in her ear, slapping her ass.

"Let's just get this over with so I can show you how gangsta I really am."

She winked and walked out the kitchen. I stood there for a minute adjusting myself before following behind her. Walking through this house and looking at all the shit that Kash and I basically paid for pissed me off even more. When we made it to Gritt's room, we could tell he was in there because the smell of fear invaded my nostrils. We walked into the cold, dark room and just sat on the bed.

"Gritt, you might as well come out because we ain't leaving no *time soon, buddy. My wife and I got all night. Ain't that right, baby?"*

"Nah, I don't have all night to be waiting on him. I'm trying to get home and fuck yo' brains out, so he might want to come out before I pay a visit to his pregnant girlfriend and make her take a nasty fall," Kash evil ass said with a smirk on her face. The mentioning of his girlfriend getting hurt triggered something inside of him because he automatically ran out the closet.

"Okay, Okay here I am. Please don't hurt my mother."

"How are you doing, Gritt?" I asked, ignoring his last statement.

"Who are you guys?"

"Who we are has nothing to do with why we are here. Why have you been stealing from us, Gregory?" Kash asked, while filing her fingernails.

"Money and Kash?" The look on his face caused me to burst out laughing.

"Answer my wife's question, man."

"I always put back what I take. Please don't kill me." Kash looked at me and nodded her head. At the same exact time, we took our masks off revealing who we really are.

"Wait... so y'all are Kash and Money?"

"In the flesh," Kash said, laughing.

"Cyn and Terran?" As soon as he said our names, we both emptied our clips inside of him. Our real identities will forever remain a mystery, because we are not those people anymore. For years we have lived in their shadows, now, now it's time for Kash and Money to shine. THIS IS OUR STORY...

CHAPTER 1

CYN

ONE YEAR AGO

"Yo sis, have you talked to Gritt?" My twin brother asked me as he walked in to the house and sat down on the couch. Not only was Jamal my twin, but he was also my best friend who I loved dearly, even though we were total opposites from each other. Jamal has always been the nice and outgoing twin, when I was the mean, blunt and antisocial sister who don't fuck with anybody.

"I haven't talked to that nigga since he left the house this morning saying that he was going to get some nigga name Terran from New York, and that was like an hour ago."

"What do you know about this Terran nigga?" Although my brother was easygoing, he could not stand the fact of new people. He might be friendly, but he has to feel you out first, and he has no problem telling you about yourself if you been fucking up.

"I don't know shit about him at all. Gritt called me yesterday talking about he has somebody who he think will be able to help us with the car lot, but I ain't fucking with nobody new."

"Especially not if Gritt's janky ass is bringing them." Gritt is our weird-ass cousin who has been in and out of jail for the past couple of years. Even though we know this nigga is living foul as shit, we know that he will never do no sneaky shit like that to his family.

"I guess we are about to find out who he is now," I said as I pointed outside and watched as Gritt walked to the door with this fine ass man, who had a menacing look on his face. I'm normally not the type of female who likes men with braids, but for some reason, it fits his light brown skin complexion and tall skinny frame. Although he had a beard, he kind of reminded me of Snoop Dogg. I have never seen a man this fine a day in my life.

"Damn Cyn, did you miss me or something?" Grit joked, trying to walk in, but I stopped him at the door. Snapping out of my lust for this man, I thought about the fact that Gritt actually brought somebody who I don't know to the place where I lay my head.

"Why the fuck would you bring somebody who we don't know to my house like you live here, Gritt?"

"He's coo, Cyn. Trust me."

"I would be a damn fool to trust you, Gritt. I'm not in the streets, but I know when and when not to trust people," I stated, looking ole dude up and down who didn't look fazed. Even though I'm not in the streets, or into the illegal business like my brother is, I grew up in the worse parts of Compton, and I had to learn how to be tough and protect my brother and me. Our parents started off with nothing, but they worked twice as hard to make sure that we had clothes on our back, food on our table, and a roof over our heads, so now it's time to take care of them.

"Look, I didn't come here to start any problems. I just recently got out of jail, and Gritt told me that he can hook me up with a job down here because he owned a car lot," Terran said, speaking his peace. Jamal and I looked at each other and burst out laughing at the bullshit that this nigga Gritt told him.

"Gritt don't own shit, sweetheart, I do, but since he sold you a false dream, I got you. What did you go to jail for?"

"My homeboy set me up, so I killed him." I quickly looked at my brother, then back to him.

"Did you snitch or something?" I asked.

"What the fuck do you mean did I snitch? It ain't a ounce of bitch in my blood." The way he answered that question let me know that he was telling the truth about that, but it wasn't just the way he answered the question. For some reason, when he first walked in the door and made eye contact with me, I felt a strange connection like I have been knowing him my whole life.

"There is no way you will be walking free right now if you killed somebody. That shit is looking a little suspect," Jamal said, giving dude the side eye while griping his gun.

"I got some people on my payroll who helped me get out, man." Jamal and I both nodded our heads understand exactly what he was saying.

"So you was a corner boy?" I asked.

"Yo ass is disrespectful as fuck, but nah, I wasn't no fucking corner boy. I ran shit down there before some niggas took over."

"So why didn't you just go back down there?"

"For what? Ain't shit left for me down there, that's why I came up here. Don't get me wrong, the streets is all I know, and I don't want to give it up, but my life is more important."

"Come take a ride with me real quick, my nigga," my brother said, getting up and walking out the room, but Terran just sat there staring at me.

"What the fuck is wrong with yo' eyes, my nigga?" I asked, getting irritated. He shook his head and laughed.

"Your mouth is reckless as fuck but sexy at the same time. I'm gone have to do something about that." He winked at me, which made my hard ass blush. No matter how many niggas I talked to in the past, none of them has made me blush.

"Yo' ass is trouble, I can feel it in my bones. I'm gone have to stay away from you."

"I think you can handle me," he said in a seductive tone, which made my kitty jump. It has never been this hard to contain myself around any nigga, but he's making it hard.

"Whenever y'all are done flirting with each other," my brother said, ruining the mood. Terran chuckled and slid me his phone. I quickly saved my number and called myself.

"My bad, bro. Yo' sister is just so fucking fine I couldn't help but fuck with her." He winked at me then started walking away.

"Yeah, ah-ight. You better watch it, my nigga," my brother threatened then walked away. I chuckled and walked out the door right along with them.

"Where are you going?" Jamal asked, while walking me to

my car.

"To pick up Nikki so we can go shopping, is that okay with you?"

"Is that where you're really going, Cyn?"

"Where else would I be going, Jamal? Nikki is my only friend, and I know for a fact mama and daddy are sleep."

"I just want to make sure that yo' ass is not slipping back into your old ways." When my brother first started selling drugs at only twelve years old, a lot of people used to fuck with him and steal his shit, so I would get all the information on the people that was fucking with him and go behind Jamal's back and kill them. My pops always taught us how to defend ourselves and each other if necessary, and everybody in Compton knows that I don't play when it comes to my money or family. Especially Jamal.

"As long as people is not fucking with you then I'm fine."

"Yea whatever. You just tell Nikki's fine ass that I will be over there today." My brother has had the biggest crush on Nikki since we were little kids, but she has not been paying him any attention at all.

"Boy please, Nikki does not want yo crazy ass." I kissed his cheek, got in my car and drove off. When I pulled up to Nikki's house, she was sitting outside smoking a blunt.

"Were you waiting on me? Don't I feel special," I joked, while getting out the car and walking up to her. She put her blunt out and mugged me.

"You need to tell yo' corny ass cousin to stop bringing his ugly ass over here trying to fuck with me," she complained, which made me crack up laughing. Her and Gritt could not get along even if it killed them. For years now he has been trying to shoot his shot at Nikki, but was severely failing at it.

"You know he is not going to listen to nobody, and Jamal said that he is coming over here today." For a second there, I could have sworn I saw a smile quickly spread across her face, but it faded when she saw me noticing it.

"What the fuck is he coming over here for?"

"To tear the lining off that pussy!" I said, screaming, making her laugh.

"You play too fucking much, Cyn, and you know damn well that Jamal doesn't really want my big ass." Nikki has always been plus size, but she never let that get in the way from living her life. She carries herself very well and don't let anything bother her. That's why I found it weird that she cared so much about what Jamal thinks of her.

"Bitch please, Jamal has been chasing after you since we were ten years old. He doesn't care anything about your weight."

"Anyways, what do you have planned for the day?"

"I was just going to chill here with you but Gritt brought this guy name Terran here from New York, and I don't want him in my house."

"Is he cute?"

"He's okay, I guess," I said, trying to downplay what he looks like.

"You know I can tell when you're lying, right?" She said with a smirk on her face.

"Okay, bitch, he is fine as fuck."

"Well fuck with him then."

"You know I don't fuck with anybody that's in the streets. I don't have time to be worried about my man and my brother."

"Bitch, you have been saying that bullshit since you been able to walk, but you need to understand that trapping is in your blood and that's who you are going to attract." What Nikki was saying was one hundred percent true, it doesn't mean that I wanted to deal with it.

"Well, I guess I'm going to be single for the rest of my life because I refuse to be up all night worrying about two niggas."

"Bitch, just a couple of months ago, you was doing the exact same thing."

"I had nothing to do with selling drugs. The only reason why I was doing what I was doing was just to protect my family. This street shit ain't in my blood." Our conversation was cut short when my brother pulled up in Nikki's driveway.

"I told yo' ass he was coming over here," I whispered in her ear, chuckling.

"God damn that nigga is fine. I thought you said that he was just okay," she shot back, catching me in my lie, but I didn't respond back because I was busy staring at Terran, who was doing the same thing.

"What are you doing here, Jamal?" Nikki said, trying to sound like she was not feeling the fact that he was here.

"I told Cyn to tell you that I was coming over."

"She did tell me, but I don't understand the point of you coming over, and who is this staring at my best friend like she's a piece of meat or something?" Terran chuckled and held his hand out for her to shake.

"My name is Terran, and you are?"

"Nikki."

"It's nice to meet you, Nikki. Cyn, can I holla at you for a minute?" I nodded my head and followed behind him.

"What's up?" I asked, leaning on my car.

"Look, I'm too damn old to be playing games, so I'm just going to cut to the chase. I wanna take you out on a date right now." I was taken back by his bluntness, but I didn't let it show. I looked away, watching as my best friend and brother walked in the house. I can't lie and say that the chemistry wasn't there between us because it was. I just didn't wanna go down that road with getting hurt again, but for some reason, I don't think that he will hurt me.

"You're driving," I responded then threw him the keys. I didn't know where we was about to go, but I was willing to take the ride.

CHAPTER 2

TERRAN

"Where are we going?" Cyn asked, not even bothering to look up from her phone. I don't know what it is, but it's something about shorty that intrigues me, like I have been knowing her for years now. I know all about her brother, and how he is the king around here, but I just didn't understand why he still hasn't put his own cousin on.

"To my house." When I said that, she instantly held her head up and looked at me with a weird expression on her face.

"I could've sworn Gritt told me that today was your first day in Compton, and the look of this house lets me know that you have been here longer than a day, so what's really going on?" I nodded my head in approval of her observant skills.

"I just wanted to feel you out before I tell you any information about me. Come in the house and make yourself at home." When we walked in the house, she stood to the side and just looked around.

"Are you going to tell me what the fuck is going on or do I have to find out myself?" She pulled a gun out of her purse and just stared at me without flinching, which I thought was so sexy.

"Chill the fuck out, killer. Basically, your brother has been thinking about expanding his business, and he didn't want to interfere with mine, so we decided to be partners, but I had to check out everybody that he is coo with."

"The only other person I know that's even on the same level with my brother is this guy named Money, and nobody is even able to get close to that nigga, so I know for a fact that you're on good bullshit." I smiled and nodded my head at her. If only she knew that she was staring directly at Money, but I love that fact that she's not stupid enough to believe anything.

14

"I work for Money." She pulled her phone out of her pocket and started cracking up. She dialed her brother's number and put him on speaker.

"What's going on, sis?"

"Does Terran check out?" She simply asked, which made him chuckle.

"Yea he good, sis. Gritt actually came through this time."

"I was just making sure. I'll talk to you later." She quickly hung up the phone and looked at me.

"So what are we doing here?"

"I didn't feel like going anywhere in particular to eat, so I decided to just bring you to my home to cook for you." She looked at me for a moment then frowned.

"You can cook?"

"It's a lot of shit you don't know about me, shorty."

"That's what tonight is for, right?" She asked, licking her lips and looking at me.

"Damn, yo' ass is just straightforward, huh?"

"That's the only way to be. When I see something I want, I just go straight for it with no regrets. I'm too old to be playing games with people." I nodded my head in agreement.

"This might sound weird and corny as fuck, but it feels like I've known you my whole life." She held her head down and blushed. I couldn't deny her beauty. Her soft yellow skin matched perfectly with her slim but thick frame, and her dimples were to die for. I have never seen a woman so perfect in my entire life until now.

"I was thinking the same exact thing; it's like I'm comfortable around you. Are we moving too fast?" She asked with a weird look on her face.

"Is there any such thing as moving too fast?" I blew out an air of frustration when my phone started ringing. I pulled it out of my pocket and noticed that it was my right-hand Derrick calling.

"What's up, D?"

"Yo Money, where the fuck you at, nigga? We got a big problem on our hands." When I looked at Cyn, she smiled and nodded her head gesturing me to go. I kissed her cheek and walked out the room.

"What the fuck do you mean we have a problem? What's going on, man?"

"Man, some niggas ran through the traps and took all of our shit." I closed my eyes and took a deep breath trying to understand what he was saying. I also didn't want to snap on him, but I'm honestly having a hard time understanding why he hasn't been on his shit. He knows that the only time I come out to handle some business is if he absolutely can't handle it. He is the only person who knows that I am Money, so when I show my face and reveal who I really am, that's how you know it's your time to die.

"I'm going to give you and the rest of the crew about thirty more minutes to figure out what the fuck is going on, and if I have to get involved, I'm killing every mother fucking body."

"Ah-ight, man." I could tell that he was frustrated with me, but I honestly didn't give a fuck. He knows that I don't like to get involved with anything unless it's necessary. When I walked back in the living room, Cyn was spread out on the couch watching tv.

"Damn Cyn, yo' ass comfortable?"

"You told me to make myself at home, so I did. Is everything okay?"

"Nah, I actually have to go, but I'll be right back."

"Wait, you expect me to stay here while you're gone?" She asked, shocked.

"Hell yeah, and yo' ass better be naked by the time I walk back in the door." I grabbed my keys and walked out, not even bothering to hear her smart ass come back. I know that we just met each other, but the feeling that I get when I'm with her is indescribable. Fuck all that getting to know each other shit; I'm going to make her mine when I get back to the house.

By the time I made it to the Dungeon, Derrick was already there waiting on me. I slid my mask on and got out the car.

"It took yo' ass long enough to get here."

"Shut yo' ass up and come on so we can get this shit over with. My girl is at the house waiting on me." He stopped in his tracks and looked at me.

"Who the fuck is yo 'girl?"

"Don't fucking worry about it my nigga, come on." When we walked down the stairs, everybody stopped talking and focused on Derrick and me. I guess they knew who I was because of the look of fear in their eyes. I pulled out a blow torch and sat down in the nearest chair while looking at everyone in the entire room.

"Who is this nigga?" One of the snakes asked Derrick while staring me down.

"Who I am doesn't matter right now. I'm just trying to figure why y'all decided to steal from the person who feed y'all?" I stated calmly, tilting my head to the side while waiting on them to say the wrong answer.

"What the fuck are you talking about, nigga? We haven't stolen shit from nobody that didn't belong to us."

"So all of my product and money that was in my trap house belong to y'all? Please help me understand how that makes sense." They all looked at each other confused until they finally realized who I was. They all started backing up and shaking their heads.

"Money?" They asked with a shaky voice. I smiled and nodded my head yes. It's something about knowing that I put fear in people's heart, that brings joys to my life.

"In the flesh, but I want to know what was that you just said about you taken shit that belongs to you again?"

"I-I-I didn't mean anything that I said, boss, I can promise you that. You know that we're loyal to you." I shook my head and started walking around them.

"You must think I'm stupid or something? I want you to

look me in the eyes and tell me that you and your boys didn't steal from me."

"No disrespect, Money, but it's going to be a little hard looking you in the eyes when you have a mask on." Derrick and I looked at each other with a smirk on our faces. I handed him the blow torch and took my mask off making sure to never take my eyes off them. When they finally saw who I was, their jaws dropped.

"Terran?"

"You see the funny thing about this whole thing is I'm the last person that anyone would expect to be Money because I'm so quiet, but those are the ones who you have to watch."

"Please just let us go, man, we promise we are not going to tell anybody or steal from you anymore," one of them cried.

"That's another thing I forgot to tell y'all. Once somebody has seen who I really am, I have no choice but to kill them because I'm trying to keep my identity a secret." Without any warning, I turned the blow torch on and burned each and every one of their bodies until the screams turned in to soft whimpers.

"I hate when yo' ass have to come out and do this shit," Derrick complained, holding his nose.

"What's wrong with you, nigga?"

"This shit stinks, man. I don't know how you can deal with the smell of burning flesh."

"I guess I'm just a nasty nigga. The feeling of torturing people is a great feeling." I picked up my gun and emptied the clip in their heads.

"Call somebody to come and clean this shit up. I'm out of here." I grabbed my keys and was walking out of the dungeon when he stopped me.

"Why are you so quick to get out of here, nigga?" His nosey ass asked.

"Didn't I tell yo 'ass that my girl was waiting on me at my house?"

"Who the hell is yo' girl? The last time I checked yo' ass

was single as fuck, but now that you met up with Jamal yo' ass... Ahhh, you must have met Cyn." I looked at him confused.

"How in the fuck do you know about Cyn?"

"Everybody in fucking Compton knows about Cyn, and how ruthless her ass can be when it comes to Jamal. She killed over five niggas because they were fucking with Jamal."

"We must not be talking about the same Cyn. She got a mouth on her, but I don't think that she is capable of killing somebody."

"Shiiit, when it came to her brother and money, she shows no remorse."

"We will see about that."

"Wait, did y'all just meet today?"

"What the fuck does that have to do with anything? When I first saw her, I knew that she was going to be my wife. You know I don't give a fuck about time and shit. I just go with the flow."

"I feel you, bro. Go home to yo' crazy ass girl." We dapped and went our separate ways. The whole way to my house the only thing that I could think about was what Derrick said about Cyn. I just couldn't believe that she could kill somebody. When I walked in the house, Cyn was in the same spot with Italian food watching tv.

"I think I can get used to this sight before me," I announced, plopping down on the couch beside her. She smiled and handed me my food.

"I didn't know what you wanted, so I just got you chicken and shrimp Alfredo."

"Good 'cause I don't really fuck with pasta like that." She turned the tv off and focused on me, making me remember what Derrick told me.

"Before you start talking, I need to ask you something, but I need you to be honest with me." She sat her food down and looked at me confused.

"Say what you need to say."

"Have you ever killed somebody before?" She looked at me for a moment then started laughing like some shit was funny.

"Why you ask me that?"

"Because somebody told me that you used to kill people who fucked with yo' money or brother, so I was just trying to figure out if that was true or not."

"Yea that's true, now what?" The way she said it let me know that her ass is actually crazy as fuck, but it was sexy to me.

"How many people have you killed?"

"I lost count, but who told you that?"

"My right-hand man Derrick."

"Well, tell Derrick if he wants to keep his lips then he better keep his mouth closed while he talking like a bitch and shit."

"That shit is sexy ass fuck, ma. Usually, I would stop fucking with a bitch who is so aggressive and hard, but you make that shit look sexy as fuck." She smiled and scooted closer to me.

"Well, I'm not your average bitch, now can I ask you the question that I wanted to before you interrupted me with bull shit?"

"Yea, go ahead, ma."

"Do you think it's weird that I want you to be my man right now?" When she asked me that question, I couldn't do anything but smile. I was thinking the exact same thing, but I didn't want to bring it up first because I didn't want to scare her off.

"I was thinking the exact same thing, baby. I feel like we can get to know each other while being in a relationship as crazy as that sounds."

"I agree. I'm the type of person to say and do whatever comes to my mind and deal with the consequences later on. The whole time you was gone I was just sitting here comfortable in someone else's home that I don't even know, which is something that I rarely do since I always have my guard up."

"Damn ma, I make you that comfortable for you to put your guard down?"

"You do actually."

"Well how about this, we take like three months to get to know each other, and after that, we take the next step." She looked at me for a minute before a big smile spread across her face as she lay under me.

"So you wanna get to know me more. I don't have a problem with diving right in to a relationship, but I agree that getting to know each other first would be better."

"Ah-ight so that's a plan, and now that we got that taken care of let's go ahead and talk about you killing people." She leaned forward to grab her food and shrugged her shoulders.

"What is there to talk about? It's not like I was walking around killing anybody who looked at me wrong, if I killed somebody, I had to have a good enough reason for it."

"I can understand that, but I'm trying to figure out if you enjoyed doing it?"

"What do you mean?"

"I mean, only a crazy person would enjoy killing somebody. So I guess I'm just trying to figure out if you're crazy or not."

"I mean, I don't like having to kill anybody, to be honest, but when somebody deserves to die, I love to torture them. It really doesn't bother me when I have to kill somebody I guess, to answer your question." I couldn't do anything but look at her sexy ass. She was literally a female version of me and didn't even notice it. I guess that's why I'm already attached to her so fast.

"Just the way I like em, crazy," I whispered as I started to rub her thigh. I can tell she was getting turned on just by the look she was giving me, but I wasn't ready to take it there with her quiet yet.

"So did you get your little situation solved?" She asked randomly.

"I guess you can say that I did. I had a couple of bitches on the team that I needed to take care of."

"Just make sure that you're not bring any snakes with you when you're teaming up with my brother. Just because I'm feeling you doesn't mean that it will stop me from killing you. If you're fucking with my brother, that means you're fucking with the way that we eat, so I have no choice but to end your life."

"Damn ma, yo' ass is serious as fuck when it comes to your brother and money, huh?"

She smirked and shook her head yes. I could respect how she felt about her brother, but I don't know how many times I have to tell her that she doesn't have to worry about me doing some shady ass shit.

"I get what you're saying, ma, but back to us. Are you staying the night with me tonight or...?"

"I like the way you changed the subject, but it's up to you. I don't have a problem with staying with you tonight; you just have to promise me that you won't try anything with me."

"Shit, I won't try nothing with you, but that doesn't mean he won't," I stated, grabbing my dick and looking at her bite her bottom lip.

"I can respect that, 'cause sometimes I can't control her either. Come show me where I will be sleeping tonight." She stood up and pulled me off the couch. I wrapped my hands around her waist and just looked at her. It turns me on at how aggressive she's being, but not too aggressive. When I pulled her in for a kiss, my dick automatically stood at attention because of how soft her lips were.

"Seems like he's already out of control and I'm still dressed, huh?" She joked.

"It ain't my fault; yo' lips are soft ass shit."

"Well, thank you, daddy, but come on so I can lay down, I'm kind of tired." I have always been open to being in a relationship, but not this early. For some reason Cyn is different from all of the other women that has been in my life. She is very open and blunt about her life, and I think that is what's drawing me to her. I don't know what the future holds for us, but I will worry about that then, right now I'm to going to bask in the moment with Cyn.

CHAPTER 3

JAMAL

"What are you doing here, Jamal?" Nikki has been giving me a hard time ever since I got here and I really don't understand why. Ever since we were little kids, I have had a crush on her, but she always gives me a hard time. She claims it's because she doesn't like me like that, but I know it's because she's insecure about her weight when it comes to me. I never understood why she feels that way about me because I love me a BBW, and her crazy ass knows it.

"What the fuck do you mean, why am I here? I can't come here to see my future wife?" Her face scrunched up as she sat on the couch.

"For one, I'm not your future wife, and I didn't invite yo' simple ass here."

"Why do you keep playing with me, Nikki? Yo' ass know you want me too, so you need to stop playing these games and keep it real with a nigga."

"I am twenty-two years old just like you, so we both know that I'm not playing no kind of games, my nigga."

"Yea, ah-ight. What do you have planned for tomorrow?" I asked, changing the subject as I went in the kitchen to fix me a plate of Lasagna.

"Cyn and I planned on going to the movies and out to eat. We will probably end up at the mall like we always do after we eat."

"I doubt that's going to happen now that her ass is all boo'd up and shit."

"How is she boo'd up when she barely knows this dude? You and I both know how Cyn is when it comes to niggas." Nikki was right about that. It's very hard for men to even get close to Cyn because of her trust issues. Her last relationship fucked her up so bad, she couldn't even leave the house for six months without her crying, and that's something that she never do.

"Did you see the way that her and Terran looked at each other when they first made eye contact? If we didn't know them, we would have thought that they been together for a long ass time."

"You're right about that one; it was like they already knew each other or some shit. That was creepy as fuck, but cute at the same time," she said, blushing like her ass was the one in the relationship.

"All I know is, he better not fuck over here or it's going to be a fucking problem." She snickered and got quiet. When Nikki and I are alone together, her ass always make the vibe weird, by being quiet and shit.

"Why do you always do that bullshit?" I wondered.

"Do what?"

"Get quiet when we are alone. Do I make you nervous?" She shook her head no and started cracking up.

"Nigga, you know damn well don't nothing make me nervous. I just don't know what to talk about, so I be quiet."

"Let's talks about us."

"There is no us, Jamal. Damn."

"Why not though, and don't say because you're not feeling me because we both know that's a lie. It's something else to it and I'm not leaving until you tell me." She sat her phone down and let out a nervous breath. I didn't want to make her uncomfortable, but I did want to know why she was so scared to fuck with me.

"Do you remember the night when I told you about me having a crush on you when we were Seniors in high school?" I looked at her for a second trying to remember, but then it clicked. I couldn't remember every single detail, but I do remember her putting a note in my locker saying that she had the biggest crush on me and she didn't want it to interfere with her friendship with Cyn.

"Yea, I remember a little bit."

"Well, when I saw you at basketball practice after school, I heard you reading the note to your friends like it was a joke or something. You told them that you would never date somebody as big as me. You were talking about me to your friends like I didn't matter." I sighed and shook my head at my own self. Back then I was a class clown and loved to do and say shit just to get attention. I was the most popular nigga in school, and I made people laugh by hurting other people, not knowing that it really affected them.

"Damn Nikki. I'm so sorry for saying that shit to you 'cause I really didn't mean any of the shit. You know that I have been feeling yo' ass way before high school."

"But that doesn't make shit any better, jack ass. That's why I won't go there with you now because I don't know if you're ashamed of me or not." Hearing her confession made me feel ten times worse than before. I will never be ashamed of Nikki and that's on my life.

"Why would I be ashamed of you, Nicole? I'm a grown ass man, who will show off my woman to any fucking body not giving a fuck what they have to say. Plus, everybody in Compton knows that you're my girl, so you can get that shit out yo' head right now."

"I'm not your woman, Jamal, and I never will be. This might sound childish, but you fucked up your chance when you talked about me in high school. Now if you don't mind, will you please get the fuck out my house?" She grabbed the plate from me and walked in the kitchen. I could tell bringing up the past got her in her feelings, so I wasn't going to stay to make her get upset. I grabbed my keys then walked out the door. I was going to leave her alone for right now, but I am determined to make her mine soon.

The feeling of someone standing over me immediately woke me up. I grabbed my gun from off the nightstand and cocked it. Once I realized that it was Gritt's dumb ass, I sat it back down and just looked at him.

"Gritt, what the fuck is wrong with you, nigga?"

"Ain't shit wrong with me. I was just waiting on you to get yo' sleepy ass up so we can get to this meeting. I was about to wake you up, but I guess you felt me standing over you."

"Don't get yo' ass fucked up, Gabriel. Now get the fuck out my room so I can get ready and where is Cyn at?"

"She's not here," he simply said then walked out the door. Once he was gone, I went in the bathroom to take a shower and brush my teeth. I slipped on some grey sweats, a white t-shirt, and my Yeezy's. Once I was satisfied with my look, I walked out my room and into Cyn's. When I saw that her bed was not messed up, I pulled my phone out and called her.

"Yes, my wonderful brother." Her ass answered on the fourth ring sounding like she was still sleep, which pissed me off.

"Where the fuck are you at, and why didn't you tell me that you wasn't coming home?"

"Chill out, Jamal. I'm at Terran house, and I didn't tell you where I was because it honestly slipped my mind. I apologize, father," she said, getting smart.

"Don't let that shit happen again, and don't forget that we are going to mama and daddy's house for dinner tonight."

"I could never forget, is that all you needed? I really want to go back to sleep."

"He's going to let you stay in his house while he is gone?" I asked, surprised.

"Yes, he is, why are you being so nosey right now?"

"I can't just ask questions about my sister's where-abouts?"

"Yes, but you're being real extra right now."

"Bye Cyn. I love yo' crybaby ass."

"I love you too," she chuckled then hung up the phone. If she would have pulled something like this with somebody else,

I would have went crazy, but, and crazy as this is about to sound, I got a feeling that she is in good hands.

"Are you ready, nigga?" I asked Gritt, who was too busy in his phone he couldn't even look at me.

"Nigga, do you hear me talking to you?"

"I heard you the first time, my nigga. I'm ready whenever you are." I just walked out the door, got in to my car and drove off. His stupid ass is going to get enough of talking to me like he's crazy. I don't understand why he wanted to ride with me when he got his own car any fucking way.

When I made it to my office building, where I conduct all my meetings with each and every one of my businesses, Terran was already there leaning on his car.

"Damn nigga, I didn't know you was getting money like this," he greeted me.

"I mean, I do what I can. Are you ready to get this over with?"

"Yea, where Gritt at?"

"I'm right here, my cousin's bitch ass couldn't wait on me, so I had to drive myself." Gritt complained as he walked up to us. I glanced at him and started cracking up laughing because he was really acting like a real life bitch right now.

"Shut yo' cry baby ass up and come on so I can get home." We all walked in to the office and was greeted by a bunch of angry faces. I know we should have told them what we were meeting about, but we just wanted to see how they was going to react and by the looks on their faces, you could tell that they were all pissed off.

"Who the fuck are these niggas and why are they in yo' shit, boss?" I couldn't even get in the room quick enough before my workers started chewing my head off.

"I don't know who the fuck you're talking to, but you need to change yo' tone before we shoot yo' ass, my nigga," one of Terran's workers shot back, aiming his gun. Terran and I just looked at each other and shook our heads.

"We need everybody to chill the fuck out. Nothing is going on, we just needed to talk to you guys before we made any decisions that concerned y'all."

"What kind of decisions and why did you tell me?" Somebody said, walking in and looking at Terran.

"Who the fuck is this coming in my shit sounding like a bitch?" I asked, getting pissed.

"This is my bro Derrick. Derrick, this is Jamal. Now if you don't mind, we were in the middle of something." Derrick chuckled and stood off to the side.

"Now like I was saying until I was rudely interrupted. Do y'all remember when I told you guys that I wanted to expand our business, but I needed to talk to someone about it because I don't like stepping on toes?" Everyone looked at me then nodded their heads.

"Well, not only are we going to expand our business, we are going to be teaming up with my nigga Terran and his crew." When I announced that, everybody looked at us weird, which I expected.

"Hold up, boss. Now I respect and trust your judgment, but we don't know these niggas and how do we know that they are going to bring in profit? The only other person I know who can bring in the same, shit probably more money us is Money and his Crew," my main man Teddy said, making me proud. Teddy has been by my side since day one, but he didn't want to be in the spotlight, so when I got big, I decided to put him in charge of finance and all of the traps which he gladly took over.

"That's because we are working with Money. Probably not directly with Money, but Terran here is very close to Money. Is everybody okay with the changes?"

"Yea, we're coo with it. Welcome to the family." Everybody shook hands and got to know one other, which is what I like to see.

"Okay, so now that we met everybody, Terran and I decided to pair y'all up so you guys can get to know both sides of

Compton. If you have any questions, you can always call or text Me, Terran, Teddy, or whoever this cry baby ass nigga is right here," I said, pointing at Terran's friend, Derrick.

"Damn nigga, you left yo' own blood out," Gritt said, sounding offended.

"Now you know damn well even if I told them to call you, they wouldn't, so chill the fuck out. Teddy will be letting everybody know who they are pairing up with. I will see everyone at the next meeting next month." I walked out the room satisfied with the conversation we just had with all of our workers.

"What are you about to get into, my dude?" Terran asked, leaning on his car.

"Probably just chill at my crib until I have to go to my parents' house later on today. Why, what's up?"

"Shit. I was just trying to see if you wanted to get out tonight or some shit."

"That's coo with me, I will hit you up when I leave my parents' house."

"Aye, so what's up with yo' sister, man?" I don't give a fuck who you are, if you bring up my sister in any way, I'm going to get defensive because I don't know what the fuck you want.

"What do you mean what's up with her?"

"I heard that she took care of some people who was fucking with you." I couldn't do anything but laugh because I know that somebody told him about my crazy ass sister.

"Is that what she told you?"

"I mean, yea, but I didn't want to believe it."

"Shit, I don't see why not. Her ass is a fucking nut and will back up anything that she says." Not only would she go crazy over me but she loves money, and if somebody steals from her or from our family, she will literally torture you until you want to kill your own damn self.

"No seriously though, she is a good person with a good heart, but if you get on her bad side, then there is no telling what her crazy ass will do."

"Yo Mal, do you have a minute?" Teddy asked with a serious expression on his face. Terran and I both nodded our heads and walked towards him.

"What's going on Teddy?"

"That nigga Gritt is moving funny."

"His ass is always moving funny, that's why I don't give his ass no authority."

"Nah, bro, it's different this time. Almost like he's trying to sabotage you and the business." Gritt was the type of nigga who wanted everything to be handed to him instead of working for it. He would rob, steal, or kill for anything that he could get his hands on and when he get caught, he would tell people that he is related to Cyn and I. It got him out of a couple of holes, but eventually a lot of people was saying that they didn't give a fuck about who he was related to. Cyn and I had to deal with a lot of bullshit that came with Gritt and we were honestly getting tired of it.

"What are you talking about, my dude?" Terran asked.

"When y'all walked out the office he started talking to that guy Derrick about how y'all are treating them wrong and the both of you are only looking out for yourselves." Terran and I couldn't do anything but laugh at his silly ass. I don't know what type of time Gritt is on, but I will end his life if he ever crossed me.

"I'm not tripping off Gritt's childish ass 'cause he ain't about this life. Make sure you watch him and ole boy closely too. No disrespect, my nigga, but just because he's your bro don't mean that I have to trust his ass."

"Shit I understand, but I can vouch for Derrick. His ass has been by my side since day one and has never switched up on me."

"We will see, but I have to get out of here before my moms starts to trip. I'll hit y'all up later." Once I got in my car, I pulled out a blunt and fired it up. Thinking about the shit that Teddy just told me has me really looking at Gritt funny now. I have put a lot of shit past him, but I don't think that I can overlook this one.

"Do you really think that Gritt would do some bullshit like that to us?" Cyn asked as we walked in to our parent's house at the same time.

"At this point, I think he would. He's probably jealous because we are adding Terran and his crew to our business and he's still not a part of anything."

"Maybe if he would act like he got some sense, then he could be a part of something. Ain't nobody in their right mind is about to put him in charge of anything when we can barely trust him. He needs to stop acting like a fucking kid."

"I know you better watch your mouth before I beat yo' butt, Cynthia," Our mother warned when we walked in the kitchen.

"My bad, mommy, I didn't know that you could hear me. Hey, daddy!" Cyn was a daddy's girl and my mother hated it. When we were little, Cyn could never get in trouble when it came to him. Everything that she did in school was anybody else's fault but hers.

"Hey, daddy's princess. How are y'all doing?"

"We good. Mama, you got it smelling good in here."

"Well, thank you, handsome, now have a seat so we can eat. Where is Gabriel at?" In my parent's eyes, Gritt could do no wrong and the only reason why they believe that is because of his parents.

"He should be on hi..."

"Ummm, why is the back door broke?" Cyn asked, interrupting the conversation. I focused my attention on the back door and noticed that the knob was barely hanging on. It looked like somebody was trying to break in honestly.

"Oh nothing that serious, baby, just a couple of teenage boys tried to break in," my father stated, not seeming to be bothered by it.

"What do you mean they tried to break in? Why didn't y'all just call us when it was happening? We literally live down the street."

"I didn't want you guys to worry about it, and plus we replaced everything that was in the shed."

"My money was in the shed, are y'all good though?" Cyn asked with an evil look in her eyes. I already knew what was about to happen, so I shoved a spoon full of Chili in my mouth trying to eat as much as I could.

"Yes, baby, we are good. You don't have to worry."

"Okay good, we will be back." Cyn grabbed me and pulled me outside.

"What are you thinking, sis?"

"That he has something to do with my cash missing, and my parents getting robbed." She nodded towards Gritt, who was pulling up in the driveway.

"Do you really think so?"

"I know so, Jamal, and he just pissed the wrong bitch off."

CHAPTER 4

CYN

I don't know what type of bitch do Gritt take me for, but he fucked up this time if he set my parents up to get robbed. Family member or not, you will lose your life over those two people and my motherfucking money. When he walked up to us with a frown on his face, I just knew that I was going to have to kill his bitch ass, which is something that I never wanted to do.

"Why are y'all just standing out here like somebody pissed in y'all cereal?" He tried to joke, but that only pissed me off even more.

"Come take a ride with us, cousin," Jamal simply said, walking over to the car and pushing him in. I slowly got in the back seat with Gritt and just stared at him trying to keep my composure.

"What the fuck is wrong with y'all?"

"We just wanted to spend some time with you, is that okay?" I tilted my head to the side and waited on him to answer.

"Man, hell nah that's not okay. Y'all up to something, man."

"You damn right we are, and you know how we roll, so I suggest you answer the question honest as fuck. Did you have anything to do with our parents getting robbed?" When I asked him that he looked at me like I just said the most disrespectful thing in the world.

"What the fuck do you mean did I set them up to get robbed! Y'all actually think I would do some foul ass shit like that to the people who fucking raised me?"

"We don't know what the fuck you would do, Gritt!"

"I wouldn't do no fucked up shit like that! Man, let me out

this fucking car before…"

"Before what, bitch?" I placed my hand on my gun waiting for him to say that wrong thing, but he just chuckled and got out the car. The way he reacted let me know that he didn't have anything to do with it, but I'm still not putting shit past him.

"You know what, I'm not even about to go there with you right now. I told the both of yall that I had nothing to do with them getting robbed, and I don't know who tried to end their life by robbing them. I know that I'm not living a good enough life, but damn I do have morals." I wanted to believe what he was saying, but at the same time, he has been acting a little different than usual. It's hard for me to believe someone who has been foul their whole life, but at the same time, my parents raised him so I know that he wouldn't do anything like that unless he was on good drugs.

"If I find out that you had something to do with my parents getting robbed, I promise I will make your life a living hell. Get the fuck out my car and walk home, bitch ass nigga." He chuckled and got out the car, slamming my door. Jamal looked at me with a smirk on his face like he just figured something out.

"Why the fuck are you looking at me like that, my nigga?"

"Let me find out that you have a soft spot for Gabriel."

"I will always have a soft spot for Gritt, that's my cousin, but I don't have a problem with ending his life for fucking with y'all or my motherfucking money." I wasn't pissed about somebody trying to rob my parents because I know that they could take care of themselves. What I was pissed about was the fact that somebody took my money, and it had to be somebody that I know or has been watching because only a few people knew where I kept my money.

"Are you going back to the house or to Terran's?" Jamal asked, stirring me out of my thoughts.

"We need to go back to mama and daddy house to look at the cameras. I'm not going anywhere until I find out who stole my fucking money."

"How much was in there?"

"The last time I checked it was over five hundred thousand in there." He stopped driving and blew out a breath.

"Who all knew about you keeping money in the shed?"

"You, Teddy, mama, daddy, and Nikki."

"It had to be somebody watching us. I'm about to text Terran and tell him to meet us at my office, so we can watch the tapes just in case he knows who they are." The mentioning of his name made a smile crept upon my face. Don't get me wrong, I'm mad as fuck about my money, but just hearing his name make my heart flutter.

The whole ride to the office my mind was going a mile a minute. Growing up in Compton was hard as fuck, especially when it came to my parents providing. It was days when we went without eating because we couldn't afford to. So when my brother and I started hustling, I vowed that I would give my parents everything they want. The feeling of having money and not worrying about anything is indescribable, so to know that somebody stole from me, is like signing a deal with the devil, and there is no coming back from that.

"Where is yo' mind at, baby?" I jumped at the sound of Terran's voice. I guess I must have blacked out because I didn't even notice that I walked into the office.

"On my fucking money, that's where it's at!" I unintentionally yelled.

"Damn, my bad, baby. I didn't mean to make you mad; I just asked a question."

"I don't like to be asked questions when I'm mad. Somebody stole my fucking money from my mama's house and we are trying to figure out who did it. My brother called you here so you can look at the cameras with us to see if you know these people."

"Ah-ight, let's go." We all walked upstairs to my brother's office, and I sat down on Terran's lap which caused him to smile and grip my thigh. When my brother turned the video on, we weren't even watching it for a good two minutes before I felt Terran tense up under me.

"What's wrong, baby?"

"Do you know them niggas, bro?" Jamal asked, catching his vibe.

"They are some of my corner boys who I just recently put on like two months ago."

"Take me to them right now." With that being said I got up, walked out the office and waited for Terran to come outside. I did not have time to be playing games with corner boys who was just looked for an easy come up. Instead of working for what they wanted, they decided to take the easy way out and steal from me.

"Listen, baby. Even though those niggas are corner boys, I teach them to be savages," Terran warned, probably thinking that shit was supposed to scare me.

"And your point for telling me that was?"

"Just because they see me with you don't mean that they are going to take it easy."

"I see I'm going to have to show you, huh? Unlock the door, so I can get in the car, it's hot out here." I don't know why Terran kept underestimating me. I'm not all bark and no bite, I will slit a bitch's throat for even looking at me wrong, but it's okay 'cause I'm about to make an example out of each and every one of these niggas.

"Why are not bringing your gun in?" I looked at Terran trying to decide if I should just ignore or curse his ass out for trying me. We were currently walking up to one of his traps, and he kept asking me these questions like I was a bitch or something.

"I think it's best if you would stop talking to her right now, bro. She don't need a gun to protect herself; I put my life on that," my brother said, defending me. When we walked in to the house, you could tell that Terran was pissed. Each and every person in there was drinking and shooting dice instead of working which set me off. I looked around and noticed that the guys that I was looking for was not in the room.

"Everybody get the fuck out of here right now, and y'all need to be in my office tomorrow 'cause this shit is unacceptable." Seeing him boss up on them made my pussy soaked. He looked back at me and winked, which made me bite my lip.

"Whenever y'all are done eye-fucking each other, those niggas are walking up here with their guns out," Jamal stated, sounding irritated which made me chuckled.

"Baby, why don't you stand behind me until I get their guns from them." I just shook my head and ignored his stupid ass. I walked over to the door the exact same time they were walking in. Before they could react, I grabbed both of their guns and hit them in the head with it.

"Now will you please stop doubting me?" I looked at Terran and smirked. In total shock, he held his hands up in surrender and backed up. Jamal and I couldn't do anything but laugh.

"I told you her ass was ruthless when it comes to her money. What do you want us to do with them?"

"Nothing, we just wait until they wake up so I can figure out where my money is." I sat on the couch and pulled my phone out. I was trying to figure out if I wanted to painfully fuck with them, or just kill them to get it over with. Feeling somebody staring at me, I looked up from my phone and noticed one of the guys just staring at me.

"Well, good morning, sunshine. Glad to see you with us today," I said in a sarcastic tone.

"Fuck you, bitch."

"Aye chill out, my nigga," Terran said, aiming his gun at dude trying to protect me.

"It's okay, baby; I got this. See, I was going to be nice and just kill you fast, so you won't have to suffer, but you just pissed me off. So, for every minute that I have to wait for your friend to wake up, will be how many body parts I cut off." He looked at me with fear then at Terran for help, but he just ignored it.

"Do you need me for anything, sis?" Jamal asked me, ignoring the situation that was currently going on.

"No, I don't, I can take care of it. I will call you when I'm on my way home." He kissed my cheek and walked out the door. Three minutes later dude's friend woke up confused about what was going on until he made eye contact with me.

"So that was three minutes, and if you multiply that by three and add one then that would be ten fingers to cut off, huh?" I asked, looking at my sexy ass man, who was giving me a look of lust.

"That sounds about right, baby."

"Please don't do this, Cyn! I'm so sorry that I stole from you," one of them cried like a little bitch.

"What's your name, son?" I leaned over and asked.

"Danny."

"Why did you and your friend steal from me, Danny?"

"We didn't know that those were your parents who lived in that house. We were just robbing them because we heard that they had a lot of money in the shed behind their house. If we knew that it was your parents, I promised we would have robbed them." Not only was I pissed that they stole from me and tried to rob my parents, I was mad because somebody close to me has been running their mouth.

"Did y'all know that the money y'all stole was from me?" They shook their heads no then held them down.

"Have y'all heard of what I do to people who steal from me? I don't play about my fucking money!" I walked in the kitchen and grabbed the biggest knife that I could find. When I walked back in the living room, both of their eyes got wide.

"P-pplease don't do this, Cyn." they begged. In one quick motion, I chopped their fingers off making blood splatter everywhere. Not satisfied with my work, I grabbed a bottle of salt and poured it on their wounds leaving them to scream to the top of their lungs.

"Do y'all realized that y'all stole five hundred thousand dollars from me! When it comes to my money, I don't show no fucking mercy. Knowing that I'm not going to be able to get my money back makes me so fucking mad that y'all cries makes me feel better. Let this be a lesson to y'all... I DON'T PLAY WHEN IT COMES TO MY CASH!" I grabbed both of their heads and slit their throats, instantly killing them. I stood there staring at their bloody bodies with a smile on my face. I hate that Terran had to see this side of me, but it's something that I had to show him too he could know not to fuck with me.

"Damn, Cyn, that shit was sexy as fuck," he said, smacking my ass and leaving me confused. I thought that I was going to run him away, but for some reason, I turned him on.

"So you're not freaked out or turned off?" I asked.

"Fuck no. This type of shit would usually turn me off, but it's sexy as fuck to watch you do it. Seeing you in this environment lets me know that I can trust you."

"What do you mean trust me?"

"I will tell you when we get to my house, do you have changing clothes?"

"Yes, it's in your car in the trunk."

"I'll be right back." He kissed my lips and walked out the door. Now that I know he won't leave me because of this, I knew that he was going to be my future husband, well depending on if this little secret he has to tell me is going to piss me off.

"So, what is this secret you have to tell me?" We have been at his house for about two hours, and he has yet to tell me this so-called secret. I don't know if I wanted him to tell me anyway because I'm actually getting comfortable with being around him. I can actually see myself moving in with him sometime soon since I am technically here all the time.

"Yo' ass just had to ruin the mood, huh?" He asked, raising his head off my lap.

"You can't just expect me to forget about what you said earlier. You either tell me, or I'm leaving." He let out a long sigh then sat up in the bed. I guess what he had to tell me was important because he took the phone out of my hand and sat it down.

"Do you remember me telling you about how I worked for Money?" He asked with a nervous look on his face.

"Yes"

"The only reason why I told you that I worked for him was because I didn't know if I could trust you, as well as not knowing if you could handle the truth."

"What are you talking in circles? Will you just come out and tell me?"

"I'm Money." I looked at him for a while trying to figure out if he was telling the truth or not, because there is no way that he could be Money. He was the most powerful man, other than my brother, in Compton, so for him to just up and say that he is Money is very hard for me to believe.

"You expect me to believe that?"

"No I don't, but I do want you to know that I'm telling the truth. I knew everything about you and your family before y'all even knew about me. The reason why I kept my identity a secret is because I wanted to make sure that you guys were legit." The look in his eyes let me know that he was telling the truth. I couldn't believe that I was actually in the same bed as Money.

"Yo' ass is really telling the truth. Do Jamal know?"

"Yea, I told that nigga a long time ago."

"Well, your secret is safe with me, and I actually think its sexy that I'm sleeping with Money." I leaned over and kissed his lips.

"What if we start our own business?"

"What do you mean?" I asked, confused.

"Like what if I give you fifty percent in all of my businesses, and I want you to be my connect. We can rule the drug world if I had my Bonnie next to me."

"You're willing to give me half of each and every one of your businesses, plus you want me to be the connect of the drug business and you barely know me?" I asked, shocked.

"It don't matter how long I've been knowing you, Cynthia, the only thing that matters to me is me trusting you. I know for a fact that we are going to be together for the rest of our lives, and I also know that you are going to do what it takes to protect everything that you care about. I'm really feeling you, Cyn, and I know that I am making a good decision." I sat there thinking about everything that Terran just said, and I honestly couldn't agree more with him. Something in my heart was telling me that he was the one who I'm going to spend the rest of my life with and I am happy about those feelings.

"I don't know the first thing to running any of your businesses, especially when it comes to drugs and shit." He looked at me then chuckled.

"I will teach and train you in everything that you need to know, baby, but you have to promise me that you will not tell anyone about this. If they find out that you are the connect, then they are going to figure out that I'm Money and they are going to come for us."

"I understand, baby, but I want a nickname too." I pouted.

"What do you mean a nickname? You got Cyn."

"I'm talking about how you're Money because you don't want people to know who you really are. If we are going to be on our Bonnie and Clyde type of shit, then we have to do this right." He ran his hands through his beard and closed his eyes like he was thinking. I can't believe that I am actually about to team up with my man to rule the world.

"What about Cash but spelled with a K?"

"Why that?" I asked curiously.

"You just killed two niggas because they stole money from you. I think the name fits because you don't play when it comes to your cash, and neither do I when it comes to my Money." When he explained why he thought that name would be a good fit for me, I sat back and smiled. Terran not only created my nickname, but he just created a monster.

"I'm feeling that a lot, baby. Kash and Money about to take over this fucking world!" He grabbed my neck and pulled me in for a deep, passionate kiss that turned me on.

"So that means that you and I are exclusive?"

"Let me show you just how exclusive we are," I whispered in his ear while straddling his lap.

"Are you sure you're ready for this dick, Cyn? It will change your life." He tried to warn, but I ignored him and took my panties off while he slid off his boxers. I reached over a grabbed the blunt off the dresser and handed it to him.

"Sit back, relax and enjoy the ride," I said in a seductive tone while sliding down on his long, thick rod. I sat there for a minute trying to adjust to his size because it was something that I have never felt before. He might have been right about me not being ready for it, but I sure was about to fake it until I make it.

"Damn," we both whispered in unison. I closed my eyes as I placed my hands on his check and rotated my hips on dick moaning softly. The feeling of him growing more inside of me drove me insane. I have never felt this much chemistry between two people a day in my life, and I think he felt it too because when I looked at him, and he was staring directly at me with his mouth open.

"This pussy is gripping my shit tight, Cyn. Shit," he growled while squeezing and lifting my ass up, so he could get better access inside of me. He held me in place as he drilled deep inside of me leaving me speechless. Never in my life have I not been able to take dick, but he was making it hard for me.

"Oh God, baby, I can't take it," I moaned as I tried bouncing up and down on his dick. Not taking his penis out of me, he lifted me up, laid me on my back, and folded my legs to my chest.

"Are you tapping out Kash? First lesson is to never back down from a challenge, so you better take this dick," he challenged, stroking me so deep the only thing I could do was bite my bottom lip, trying not to tap out.

"This shit is so fucking addicting, Cyn. Damn."

"I'm about to cum!" I was able to scream out while shaking uncontrollably. He started picking up his pace, going longer and deeper, eventually sending me over the edge and squirting all on his sheets. By the time I was able to come down off of my high, I looked over and saw that he was halfway sleep. As cute as he was right now, I was not able to sleep on some wet ass sheets.

"Terran, get up so I can change the sheets," I said, shoving him.

"Yo ass can't put it on me that good and expect for me

to have some energy," he complained while getting out the bed and helping me change the sheets.

"I'm going over to Nikki's house sometime tomorrow, so she can do my hair, is that okay with you?"

"Yea that's fine, just make sure that it's not in the morning because I want you to go to this meeting with me."

"What meeting?"

"I am going to introduce you as a partner in the business and I want everyone to know."

"Don't you think they will know who I am if they hear my voice?" I asked, kind of confused.

"Not if you change it up a tad bit, and I know that your brother doesn't let you go around his workers, so they shouldn't really know what your voice sounds like."

"That's true, but I have a very distinctive voice and every-body is going to know who I am."

"Well, change it up. I'm about to go to sleep though." I guess that was my cue to end the conversation 'cause he pulled me down on the bed with him and laid between my legs. I didn't know how tomorrow was going to go, but I was somewhat ready for it.

I have never been nervous a day in my life, but today is different. Sitting behind a very thin wall, looking at all of the people who work for Jamal and Terran was a bit intimidating, and I have a feeling that they are not going to like the fact that a woman is going to be telling them what to do.

"Okay okay, we need everybody to settle down for a minute," Jamal said, clapping his hands like he was talking to some middle schoolers.

"How can we calm down? Did you hear about what your sister and Terran did to Danny and Harvey?" One of the workers said.

"Yea I heard what they did, and they had every reason to do what they did. Danny and Harvey stole from them and they had to pay for it."

"Where is Terran anyways? He is never here when we have meetings."

"Are you questioning yo' boss' loyalty?" Derrick asked while stepping closer to the guy.

"Hell yea I am and I don't give a fuck. How come he is always late or not here when we have meetings, but Money chose him out of all people to partner with him?" Jamal shook his head and chuckled.

"You just wrote a check that yo' ass can't cash."

"What the fuck do you mean by that?" He asked, confused.

"Derrick, you go and take care of him while I get this meeting started. I got other shit to discuss than to be worried about a nigga who just stuck his foot in his mouth. I don't understand why niggas think it's okay to question my choices in my own damn business," Terran… well, Money said, making his self-known. The way he just took over and had these niggas shook had me ready to just fuck him right now. The power that he has is such a turn on.

"Does anyone else have a problem with how I run things?" When nobody else said anything, he smiled and started talking again.

"Now that we have that out the way. There are some things that I like to address. Not that I have to explain myself, but the reason why Terran is barely here is because I have him take care of some things that only he can do, that's why I have Derrick here. I do want to let everyone know that you guys are doing a wonderful job at making money. The next thing I want to bring to your attention is how busy I have been lately and it's starting to take a toll on me."

"So what are you saying? You're about to retire?" Somebody yelled out, sounding depressed or like the world was about to end.

"There is no such thing as me retiring when it comes to this shit. What I was trying to say before I was rudely interrupted is that I decided to bring somebody on as my partner in all of my businesses, and this person will also be our new connect."

"So who is it?" Jamal asked, confused.

"Now before I introduce this person to everyone, I need you guys to give her the same respect that you give me. Not only is she my partner in this business, but she is also my woman, and she deserves respect."

"So what's her name?" Jamal asked with a smirk on his face already know who it was. Terran looked at me and nodded letting me know that it was my turn to speak.

"My name is Kash with a K, and I am so happy to be a part of this team. I really don't have anything to say, just don't underestimate me just because I'm a girl. I need you guys to fear me just like y'all fear Money. Do you guys have any questions for me?" I guess everybody was stuck in their own world because they didn't say anything, they just nodded their head in agreement.

"Well now that we got that taken care of, thank you so much for coming, Kash and Money. I need everybody else to stay a little later so we can take care of some business," Jamal ordered everybody. Terran and I got up and walked out the door hand in hand. I'm so glad that the meeting went well, because I really didn't feel like killing anybody.

"Are you about to go to Nikki's house?" He asked once we got in the car.

"Yea and I'm probably not going to come over tonight because I haven't spent time with my best friend in a long time."

"I'm going to sit here in the back listening on their conversation, just call me when you get to the house." I kissed his lips, got in the car, and drove off. I can't believe that I am actually about to be a connect, and part owner of Terran's business. Cyn has been running the streets putting fear in many hearts, but now it's time for Kash to shine.

CHAPTER 5

NIKKI

"I'm just trying to figure out what took yo' ass so long to get here?" I turned my nose up at her when she plopped down on the couch and rolled her eyes like she had an attitude.

"Ewwww, bitch, don't be bringing any negative vibes in my house. What the fuck is wrong with you?"

"Nothing is wrong with me. I just miss my man, that's all."

"Bitch, you just got over here, and we haven't even seen each other in a long time. Ever since you got yo' little man, you have not been hanging around me lately. Don't forget who raised yo' buckethead ass."

"Bitch, please calm yo' ass down. I miss my man, but where am I at right now? With you so calm yo' ass down, little dookie." I snatched her hat off her head and ran my fingers through her rough hair.

"What do you want me to do to this mess that's on your head?"

"You can just give me a silk press, and I already washed it, but I have a question." I looked at her and noticed that she had a serious expression on her face. I was in a good mood and I had a feeling that the question she was about to ask was going to mess it up.

"If it's something that's going to piss me off then just save it."

"I don't know who you think you're talking to like that, but you better simmer down some."

"Cyn, please stop playing with me. What do you have to ask me?"

"Why don't you want to give my brother a chance?" I let out a sigh of irritation and shook my head.

"Can we talk about your relationship with Terran instead?"

"I will talk about that after you tell me what is wrong with my wonderful brother?" I rolled my eyes at the fact that I knew she wasn't going to let this go. Cyn is my best friend in the whole wide world, and she will always fight for me no matter what the situation is, but when it comes to her brother, it's like pulling teeth trying to get her to understand my point. That's why I never told her about what he said to his friends about me.

"I just don't want to fuck with him like that."

"Why not though? There is nothing wrong with my brother at all."

"Because if we was to ever take it there, then I know that he would be ashamed to be seen with me, Cynthia."

"Why are you insecure when it comes to him, Nikki? Everybody knows how Jamal feels about you, and he will never do anything like that."

"When we were in high school, I overheard him talking about me to his friends after I finally build up the courage after all those years to tell him that I liked him. He stood there and talked about me like I was a fucking dog and that fucked it up for him 'til this day." She looked at me for a second trying to figure out if I was telling the truth, then a weird look came upon her face.

"Why didn't you tell me this when it happened?"

"You know how you are when it comes to Jamal."

"How am I?"

"You act like he could do no wrong in your eyes, but he did when we were seniors. That's why I never wanted to tell you, I didn't feel like hearing you come up with excuse for him," she chuckled and shook her head from side to side like I offended her, but I honestly didn't give a fuck.

"I can't lie and say that I don't take his side with most things, but he was wrong in that situation and I don't blame you for feeling the way you feel."

"But..." I replied, already knowing that she had something else to say.

"But I do think that he genuinely likes you, and has grown up from the clown that he used to be."

"He would really have to prove that to me in order for me to at least give him a shot." I looked at her and she had a sneaky smirk on her face.

"Wait, so you still have feelings for Jamal?"

"They never left, I just didn't want to act on those feelings because I don't trust his ass."

"I think you should just give him a chance before it's too late. We all know that Jamal was a fucking clown at first, but I think he has changed. He has been having a crush on you since we were like five years old and that haven't changed at all." I understood what she was saying, but I still don't know about giving him a chance. Even though I wasn't paying him any attention our whole life, he has not been with a female exclusively in a long time, and that's what I liked about him.

"I will think about it, but this conversation will stay between us only. I will do this on my own time and not yours, okay?"

"Fine, but I need you to hurry up so I can have some nieces and nephews." I couldn't do anything but laugh at her silly ass.

"Oh, bitch, settle down. I don't plan on having kids until I'm about twenty-six, so I got about four years. Anyways, what's going on with you and Mr Terran?" The smile that was plastered on her goofy ass face let me know that he is making her happy.

"If I tell you something, you have to promise me that it is going to stay between us."

"Bitch, who else am I going to tell when you're my only friend?"

"Don't get smart with yo' raggedy ass, but I'm serious, Nikki. The shit that I'm about to tell you is on some top-secret shit, and if you tell somebody, then I will have to kill you." The look on her face let me know that she was being serious about what she just said. I know I should feel offended about her threating to kill me because she tried to play me, but it only intrigued me more.

"I'm not going to tell anybody, Cyn. You have my word."

"You know Money, right?"

"Bitch, who doesn't know Money? He is the most feared but respected man in the City of Compton. I bet you he is ugly as fuck, but his power makes all the bitches wet." That last statement must have triggered something in her mind because she closed her eyes and bit her bottom lip.

"Where did yo' mind just go, Cyn?"

"Money isn't ugly," she responded back.

"And how in the fuck do you know that?"

"Because Terran is Money, and Money is Terran." I kind of figured that he was very close to Money because of the powerful vibe that he gave me when I first met him, but I would have never thought that he would be Money.

"Are you serious, Cyn?"

"As a fucking heart attack."

"I kind of figured that he was something important. I just never thought that he would be Money because he is too fucking quiet and laid back for that shit."

"That's exactly why nobody knew that he is Money." She smirked and looked at me like she was a proud parent. I couldn't believe that her ratchet ass was actually fucking with The Infamous Money.

"Damn, Cyn, and you're actually coo with all of this?"

"Why wouldn't I be?"

"Because you're always the one that's going around saying that you don't want to be with a hood nigga and all that bullshit."

"Well, it's something about Terran that attracts me to him. This man even told me that he's giving me fifty percent of all his business, including the illegal ones."

"Bitch, you don't know nothing about the streets," I responded back while chuckling. Cyn might be a killer, but she doesn't know the first step when it comes to the drug games.

"I know I told him that, and he told me that he is going to

train me in to being his Queen."

"So y'all are basically on some Bonnie and Clyde type of shit, huh?"

"Nah, we're on some Kash and Money type of shit." I can tell that Terran really makes Cyn happy, I just hope that he is not trying to play my best friend, or he is going to see the ugly side of me.

"Aye! I'm feeling the fuck out of that shit, sis! You're making mama so proud."

"You sure do know how I kill the vibe. Come on and do my hair so we can go out tonight. I feel like I need to be celebrating something." I was down to go out tonight since we haven't done anything with each other in a minute. For the next couple of hours, I just talked to Cyn while I did her hair.

"It's packed as fuck in there, Cyn, do you think we should just go to another club?" I asked, trying not to kill the vibe. I wasn't a big fan of females, and if there are too many of them bitches around, I start to feel like I have to fight.

"Um, bitch, no. Plus we can get a V.I.P table in here for free now come on." She grabbed my hand and pulled me to the front on the line and had all the ratchet bitches in their feelings.

"Just because Jamal is her brother doesn't mean that they can just go to the front of the line," one of the ratchet bitches said which we decided to ignore. The bouncer chuckled, gave us a hug and just let us in without any problems.

"That bitch and her friend can't get in here. I don't want any problems tonight if you understand what I'm saying."

"I got you, Cyn; you two just have a good night. Oh, Cyn, your brother, Terran, and some of their friends are in there just to warn you." The smile I was once wearing was cut short and the mentioning of Jamal. It was not that I didn't want to see him, because I did, I just didn't know how he was going to act because he was around his friends, but I wasn't going to worry about that right now.

"Did you know that he was going to be here?" I asked Cyn, who had this devilish smirk on her face.

"I can't hear you; the music is too loud," she responded and started walking away. When we made it to our area, Cyn's in love ass left me at the table by myself for Terran. I looked across the room at Jamal and this chick who was all in his face. I really wasn't tripping that hard off of it because I caught him stealing glances at me.

"Why are you sitting over here by yourself, thickems?" I rolled my eyes at Gritt as he sat down next to me. Gritt was not a bad looking guy at all, he was actually fine as ever, but his evil ways mad him ugly as fuck. I don't understand why he tries to talk to me knowing how Jamal feels about me.

"Why are you over here talking to me, Gritt?"

"You look like you needed someone to talk to so I thought I would be the lucky someone."

"No offense, Gritt, but I don't think that she's fucking with you like that." I looked up from my phone and noticed that this dark skin sexy nigga was standing over me with a smirk on his face.

"Well, shit my bad, I was just trying to be a good friend." When he got up and walked away, I couldn't do anything but laugh.

"Thank you so much for making him leave."

"You're welcome, shorty. I could tell that you really didn't want to talk to him."

"I'm Nikki and you are?" I held my hand out waiting for him to shake it and tell me his name.

"I'm Derrick; it's nice to meet you, beautiful. Why are you over here by yourself?"

"Well, I was supposed to be here with my best friend, but she ditched me for her man."

"Who is your best friend?"

"Cyn." His facial expression changed when I said that she was my best friend. It was like she made him mad or something.

"I didn't know that was your best friend. Well, in that case, I can keep you company because she's not going to leave that nigga's side all night."

"Are you coo with Terran?" I asked.

"That's my right hand," he simply said, which let me know that he was jealous of Cyn. I felt somebody staring at me and saw that it was Jamal with a mug on his face. I rolled my eyes and focused on the man who actually wanted my attention.

"Well, it looks like we were going to meet eventually, huh?" I flirted to change the subject. He smiled and handed me a drink that he had by his side. Now any stupid bitch would accept the drink that he gave them because it was free, but I'm smart enough to know not to drink anything that a stranger gives me in a club.

"I got you a drink on me."

"Thank you, but I think I'm going to stay sober tonight and plus, the pill haven't dissolved yet," I laughed and pointed to the drink that had a pill slowly disappearing in the drink. He laughed and ran his hands down his face.

"I guess I'm caught, huh?"

"I guess so, and I think it's best if you just get up and walk away before you get yourself killed." I tilted my head to the side and nodded my head towards Jamal, who was walking toward us. I could tell he was mad because his vein looked like it wanted to pop out the side of his neck.

"I fucked up this time, but you will be mine, ma," Derrick whispered in my ear sending a warning chill down my spine. I should have known that he wasn't shit when he first came over here and talked to Gritt like they were friends.

"What the fuck was that all about, Nikki?" Jamal yelled, yanking me out of my seat.

"Why are you grabbing me like this, Jamal, and who the fuck are you yelled at like that?"

"Why was that nigga Derrick all in your face, and did he slip something in your drink?"

"Drink it and see?" I shot back, grabbing the drink and trying to get him to drink it, but he aggressively grabbed the drink and threw it on the ground. I knew for a fact that Jamal was not drunk, because he's not a heavy drinker, so he must have been real mad to show his ass in front of everybody.

"Nikki, you're really pissing me off right now. Why the fuck was you talking to him?"

"Why does it matter who I was talking to?"

"He slipped something in your drink!"

"First of all, I need you to bring it down a couple of notches before you get your feelings hurt. Second of all, I know that he slipped something in my drink because I saw it floating. I'm not a stupid bitch, Jamal. You're really starting to piss me the fuck off."

"What is going on here? We could hear y'all yelling from across the room?" Cyn asked concerned while walking over to the both of us with Terran not too far behind.

"Yo' brother think he's scaring somebody."

"Nah, yo' best friend is over here accepting laced drinks from a nigga who is about to die."

"The only person who I saw over here talking to you is Derrick and Gritt, and I know for a fact that Derrick wouldn't do know shit like that to anybody, especially my woman's best friend," Terran said, trying to defend Derrick which pissed me off.

"And I know for a fact that Gritt wouldn't do no shit like that because he has been trying to get me since we were little, and he has never done no bullshit like that no matter how desperate he is. Plus, Derrick even admitted to doing that bullshit. He doesn't even like Cyn." Terran looked at me like he was shocked that Derrick did something like that to me, but he needs to be worried about him not liking his woman right now.

"Go to my house and wait for me there, baby. I'm going to go and talk to Derrick about this shit. I don't know what type of time this nigga is on, and I'm sorry, Nikki." He gave me a hug and walked out the club. I looked at Cyn, and she was contemplating on if she should leave or stay here. Jamal spoiled my mood, so I was honestly ready to go, but I was not about to leave her if she wasn't ready to go.

"What do you want to do, Cyn?" I asked.

"If you're ready to go then you can leave, I will probably stay and chill with Teddy and Gritt."

"Are you sure?"

"Positive, I will call you in the morning. Wait... how are you getting home?"

"Jamal is going to take me since he ruined my mood." He quickly looked over at me with a mean mug like I said something wrong.

"Who said I was gone take you home?"

"You don't have a choice, little daddy, so gone over there and say bye to your friends, and that little bitch who look like she wants to beat my ass right now. I will be outside in the car." I snatched the keys out of his pocket and just walked away. I don't know what I was mad about the most, the fact that he was entertaining another bitch, or the way he just acted when we were in the club. When I made it outside, Terran was leaning on Jamal's car looking like he wanted to murder somebody.

"Why are you looking like something stinks out here?" I asked, walking up on him.

"What did you mean when you said that Derrick didn't like Cyn?"

"As soon as I said that I was her best friend, he made this face like he was jealous of y'all relationship or something."

"Now that you're mentioning it, that nigga has been acting funny since I have been with her and hanging out with Jamal."

"Yea, and he's the only nigga dumb enough to trust Gritt. I know that's your boy, but you need to watch your back, sir. Something about him isn't right."

"I know and I'm about to find out what it is. I know this is not my business, but I think you should give my nigga a chance." It was cute how he tried to vouch for his friend, but I really was not trying to hear that right now.

"Don't be trying to take up for your little friend."

"I'm just saying, if we are not talking about business then he's talking about you." He winked then walked away leaving me standing there confused. I really didn't have a good reason as to why I wanted to stay away from Jamal except for me being selfish.

"Get yo' funny looking ass in the car being friendly and shit," Jamal fussed while snatching the keys out of my hand and getting in the car. Terran and I both looked at each other then burst out laughing.

"I'm going to let you go before your man has a bitch fit. We need to set up a time for us to hang out so we can get to know each other better since I'm marrying your best friend."

"Nikki, get yo' ass in the car before you be walking!" I closed my eyes and counted to ten before I got in the car with him. Seeing Jamal like this is kind of weird, because it is very rare that he gets mad, hell even irritated. I waved goodbye to Terran and got in the car without saying two words to him.

"You wanna go home or go over my house?" He had the nerve to ask.

"Why am I going home with you tonight? Cyn is not there, we aren't fucking, and you are not my man."

"You keep talking out the side of yo' neck and you're going to get fucked up."

"Yea whatever, Jamal. Just take me home please." Instead of responding, he just turned the radio up and drove to his house like I knew he was. My phone was ringing, and when I pulled it out to see who it was, I just rolled my eyes and put it back in my purse.

"Who is that, your sister?" He asked, giving me the side eye.

"Yep."

"Why didn't you answer?"

"I didn't feel like it, and you know the only thing she wanted to tell me was how her and mom went out to eat and how I wasn't invited. I'm not trying to hear that right now." I love my mama and sister to death, but they can be real shady sometimes. Ever since I was little, my older sister has always been her favorite just because she hated who I hung around. She was not a big fan of Cyn and her family because unlike us, they grew up poor and my mama thought that we were better than them. When she found out that I was actually going over there and spending more time with Cyn's family instead of my own, she started acting like she was better than me and started treating my sister better than me. I didn't care at all, it just got annoying when I started getting older.

"No offense, but your family is childish as fuck."

"I know, that's why I don't fuck with them like that. Why is it so fucking cold in here tonight?" I complained as we both walked in his house.

"'Cause I knew that you were coming home with me tonight."

"What are you talking about, negro?"

"I remember when we were little, and how you would get out the bed with Cyn and climb in bed with me when you got too cold, so I thought that I would turn the heat down to sixty, you would get in the bed with me." I couldn't do anything but smile at how slick this bastard was. He was right about one thing though. I hate being cold and I will do anything just to stay warm.

"That was real cute what you just did." I went in Cyn's room, grabbed some of my sleep clothes that I keep over here, changed and went back in to Jamal's room. I climbed in his bed and snuggled close to him.

"Yo' ass confuse me, shorty."

"What do you mean?" I asked while looking at him.

"You claim that you don't want me, but here you are in bed with me laying on my chest."

"It's complicated, Jamal."

"How in the fuck is it complicated, Nikki? I understand that I fucked up in the past, but haven't I proved to you that I've changed?"

"You did, but I'm scared that you're going to change your mind one day." He shook his head and chuckled.

"I have never been so sure about anything in my life,

Nikki. I have had feelings for you for a long ass time, and if I wasn't sure about them, then I wouldn't have been so persistent on getting you. I'm a grown ass man, and I don't have time to be playing games with you." I thought about what he was saying, and he was honestly telling the truth. He has been showing me that he is serious about being with me for a long time now. Maybe it's time for me to realize that I have been the holding on to something so old.

"Fine! I will give us a chance, but we have to take it slow. We can't be all in love and shit like your sister and Terran is right now. My feelings for you have never went away, and it's sad that it took me so long to realize that." He grabbed my face and kissed me passionately, making me weak. I have dreamed about this moment for a long time, and the fact that it's finally happening means the world to me. I guess I didn't realize that I really wanted to be with him until I was actually with him.

"You don't know how long I have been waiting for this day, shorty. I'm going to make sure that I never hurt you intentionally." We were both interrupted by his business phone ringing. I sighed and just rolled over already knowing that he was about to leave.

"What's going on, Terran? Wait... what? I'm on my way right now." He hung up the phone, got out of bed and threw on some clothes.

"Be careful out there."

"This is what I do, baby. I'm always careful when I'm handling business."

"You heard what I said. When are you going to retire anyways?" He pulled me up from the bed and wrapped my arms around his waist.

"I'm never going to retire; I'm trapping for life, ma. You just make sure that you're here when I get back okay?" I nodded my head and kissed his lips as he walked out the door

CHAPTER 6

GRITT

"Have you lost your fucking mind, Derrick?"

"Hell nah, I haven't lost my mind. You was the one who told me to try to get closer to Cyn and what better way to get closer to her then to go through her best friend." Derrick and I was sitting at my house discussing how he just fucked up at the club tonight.

"I told you stupid ass that you can fuck with anybody but Nikki, my nigga! That's my bitch and she is off limits."

"So you're saying that you would kill me over fucking with her fat ass, but you wouldn't kill me for fucking with yo' own damn blood? Yo' ass is really cold hearted." He shook his head and continued to roll up the blunt. I know I'm coldhearted, but I honestly don't give a fuck when it comes to Cyn and Jamal. They both walk around like they run Compton, and like they don't give a fuck about me but be demanding respect all the time. I love and appreciate my family for taking me in when my parents died, but those are some dirty mother fuckers, and I'm determined to take them down.

"I stop giving a fuck about them when they decided to let a fucking stranger in the family business instead of me."

"Aye look, I'm all for killing Cyn and Jamal but we are not killing Terran, and that's not up for discussion." I looked at him and just laughed. I wasn't going to let him know that I already have a plan to kill Terran because I still need his help with taking care of my family, but as soon as I'm done with him, then he is going to die right along with his little friend.

I originally didn't have a problem with Terran until he started hanging out with Jamal and took my spot. It also bothers me how he just be walking around thinking that he has all the juice just because he is working for Money. Our conversation was interrupted when my phone rang. I instantly got irritated when I looked at the phone and saw that it was Jamal calling.

"What's up, cuz?"

"Where are you at?" I could tell in his voice that he was pissed about something which I already knew was about what Derrick tried to do to Nikki.

"The crib, what's going on?"

"Can you meet me at my office like now?"

"I'm on my way."

"Make sure you come alone, my nigga." That was the last thing he said before he hung up on me which is another reason why I don't fuck with him like that.

"What was that all about?" Derrick asked me. I just grabbed my keys and walked out the door, not bothering to respond to him. He was really starting to piss me off thinking he can question me about shit that is not his business. I don't know what Jamal wanted; I just hope that it was not any bullshit.

"Is everything good, Jamal?" I asked, trying to sound concerned when I walked in the building. When I looked next to him and saw Cyn and Terran, I knew that it was about to be some problems.

"Have a seat for me, cousin. I need to talk to you about some shit." I chuckled and sat down directly in front of Terran making sure to not break eye contact with him.

"Why did y'all call me here?"

"Do you remember when we asked if you had anything to do with our parents almost getting robbed, and somebody stealing all of Cyn's money from the shed?" On the inside I was laughing my ass off because I was the one who told my little niggas about the money in the shed. Shit, I'm still spending the money, but I didn't tell them to rob my auntie and uncle.

"Yea I remember, what about it though?"

"Well, when I left the club it was brought to my attention from Teddy that one of the guys who you hang out with knew the men who actually was the ones who took my money," Cyn said, looking like she wanted to murder me.

"Okay, but what does that have to do with me?" She held her head down and laughed which is something that she does when she is trying to control her temper.

"It has everything to do you, Gritt. How in the fuck did your people find out where my parents lay their heads, and where my money was located? You better watch what the fuck you say, because your life depends on it, my nigga." I didn't pay no mind to that empty threat that Cyn just said to me because we both know that she is not going to do nothing. Cyn might act all hard, but when it comes to family, she will always have a soft spot for the kid.

"Yea whatever. Like I told y'all before I had nothing to do with that, so y'all need to stop asking me that shit. Maybe y'all have been slipping lately when it comes to y'all security. Seems like it's y'all fault." I guess I was feeling myself a little too much because the next thing I felt was a bullet tearing through my arm.

"Ahh shit!" I screamed, grabbing my arm and looking at Terran, who was walking towards me with the look of death. I looked over at Cyn and Jamal hoping that they would help me, but they had a smirk on their face like they wanted it to happen.

"You have been walking around like you are untouchable because of those two right here, but that stops today. I know all about you and Derrick teaming up for some dumb reason, but I called you here to warn you. I suggest the both of y'all hold off on y'all little so-called plan before it get y'all killed. You have been giving too many chances with your life, but that stops now. The next time I hear anything about you or Derrick trying to pull some slick shit, I'm not wasting any time putting a bullet in the both of y'all head. Do you understand me?"

I looked at all of them and smirked, because they don't know that they just made it ten times worse for all of them. I'm tired of always being targeted and not appreciated by my family but for them to actually stand there as I get shot by somebody else, just let me know that I'm making the right decision.

"Y'all are some funny sons of bitches, but I'm going to respect y'all wishes and stay away from y'all." I just laughed and walked out the door, not bothering to wait for their response. When I made it to the car, I pulled out my phone and placed Derrick on speaker.

"You still don't want me to take care of Terran, bro?" The whole time I was in there with them, I made sure that Derrick was on the phone with me so he can hear everything that I was being told.

"Do what you have to do, my nigga. I'm just ready to get this shit over with."

"We are going to have to put a pause on our plan because they are going to be watching us very close, and I have to try to gain Jamal and Cyn's trust back."

"And how in the fuck do expect to pull that off?"

"I'm just going to have to act like I'm loyal to them for like a month or two, but while we are doing that, we are going to be building up our own team." He was quiet for a moment probably trying to process everything that I just said.

"Man, ah-ight. You just better hope this shit works."

"It will, my nigga, just trust me. I will talk to you when I leave the hospital." It was going to take a miracle to get my family to trust me again, but I think if I am consistent with it then I could do it. I just couldn't wait until they were on the other end of my gun begging for their lives like the bitches they are.

CHAPTER 7

TERRAN

ONE MONTH LATER

It has been a month since I had a conversation with Derrick and it was honestly driving me crazy. I just don't understand how he could be so cold to someone who has been by his side since we were little niggas stealing candy out the store. Not to mention this bitch ass nigga had to nerve to team up with Gritt to try and kill me, that's what really fucked me up.

"Kash, where are you at?" I yelled while walking in the house. The past month I have been training Cyn on how to properly be in the drug business, as well as being cutthroat and heartless at the right now. It honestly didn't take a long time because she has it down to a T now, I be catching myself calling her Kash all the time now.

On top of being my Trap Queen, she is amazing when it comes to our relationship. She is all that I have ever wanted in life. I can't believe that after only two months of being together I am in love with her. It's like we have been knowing each other all of our lives.

"I'm in the kitchen, baby!"

"What are you in here cooking?" I wrapped my arms around her waist and kissed her cheek.

"Nothing major, just burgers and fries. Jamal and Nikki are about to come over here, and I wanted to feed them."

"Are you ready for your first meeting tomorrow?"

"Yes and no. I'm not used to you being at the meeting with me."

"I'm still going to be there, baby; I'm just not going to be by your side. You know that Money does not go to reup meetings."

"I know, but how am I going to tell them that Derrick is no

longer apart of the business anymore?"

"Just how you just said it. Baby, everybody on the team respects you just as much as they respect me, and they know that whenever we make drastic decisions like this, it's always a good reason behind it. Now I'm going to have to figure out how in the world am I going to act like I care about this nigga being off the team."

She looked at me and chuckled. When it comes to my business, I show no remorse for anybody who tries to sabotage everything that I worked hard for, so me actually having to act like I'm really hurt by losing Derrick as one of my employees is going to be extremely hard. On the other hand, losing him as a friend is very hard for me to deal with because he has been by my side since day one, and it's going to be weird as fuck not having him around.

"Well, I know that's going to be hard, but don't you think you should talk to him or something?"

"Why am I talking to him, Cyn?"

"Because that's your best friend, and you can't just throw him away like that."

"So if you found out that Nikki was teaming up with somebody who wanted you dead, you wouldn't want to kill her?"

"Of course I would, but that doesn't change that fact that people can change, Terran. Yea it's really fucked up what Derrick tried to do, but you don't think he was being brainwashed by my cousin?"

"Nah, I don't think that because he is too smart to let other people think for him. He had to make this decision on his own, and I want to know why."

"Well, don't you think you should talk to him?"

"Talk to who?" I turned around and saw Jamal and Nikki walking in the kitchen. Now that we are all family, I decided to give him a key to my place for emergencies only. Not to mention the fact that he's been over here literally every day since Cyn moved out of their place about two weeks ago.

"I told him that he needs to have a conversation with Derrick just to understand why he wanted to kill him," Cyn answered, hugging him.

"I can tell him that. He wanted to kill you because he was jealous of your relationship with Cyn."

"Why would he be jealous of her?" I asked, confused.

"I told you why he was jealous when we were at the club, Terran. He probably don't want to get used to the fact that you're in a relationship now and he has to share you," Nikki said, putting her two cents in. Jamal and I both looked at each other frowning.

"That's some gay ass shit, Nikki."

"But it's the truth, T, and you know it. Like when you and Cyn first started hanging out, I was so mad and jealous that I had to start sharing my best friend with somebody else when it's usually been just me and her. I couldn't stand yo' stupid ass at first, but I had to realize that she was happy and I can't stand in the middle of that." Nikki was making sense, but I still refused to believe that Derrick was out here acting like a straight bitch.

"Anyways, Nikki and I are about to go upstairs so I can talk to her in private, the food is ready whenever y'all are ready to eat." I smacked her ass and leaned over so I could peck her lips before they walked away.

"I would really appreciate it if you would not do that freaky shit in front of me," Jamal complained while fixing his plate.

"So, are you going to be at the meeting tomorrow?"

"You know I will. Money don't show up to meetings unless he have to."

"So who are you thinking about to replace Derrick?"

"I was thinking about your boy Teddy?" Even though I do not know Teddy like that, I'm pretty sure that he will do what he have to do to make sure that everything is straight, and he seems like a pretty legit dude.

"I was thinking the exact same thing, nigga. Teddy has been loyal to me since I first started this shit, and I think it's time that he is standing besides the both of us, running shit."

"Do you think we should tell him about Kash and Money?" I am very particular on who knows about me and Cyn being Kash and Money because you never know who can't hold water. Although Derrick did me dirty by trying to kill me, I know for a fact that he will never tell a soul about who I really am.

"Let's just feel him out to see how he is going to handle this new position first. I trust Teddy with my life, but I will hate to have to kill him for running his mouth." I nodded my head in agreement. I usually don't like to put my business in the hands of a stranger, so I will probably meet up with him before I make any drastic decisions.

"Call him and see if he's available for a meeting with us tomorrow just so I can get a feel of him."

"Tomorrow when?"

"Probably after I pop up on Derrick so I can have a chat with him. That will probably be around three."   I didn't feel like I should even be having a conversation with Derrick, but I can't lie and say that I didn't want to know why he decided to do what he did because I really do.

"Why does it sound like y'all are talking business instead of bonding with each other?" Cyn asked, sitting on my lap and kissing my lips.

"Why should we be bonding, Cyn?"

"Umm because he is going to be your brother in law soon, and I want you guys to have that brotherly connection." Jamal and I both looked at each other before bursting out laughing.

"If you don't sit yo' ass down somewhere, Cyn. Terran and I bond through business. We are not about to go to the mall and out to eat like y'all females do. That's some gay ass shit."

"Speaking of bonding, I forgot to tell you that my mama was coming over here today to meet my woman," I mentioned to Cyn, who looked like she wanted to kill me. My mama called me early this morning fussing about how I have not came to see her, and how I'm in a relationship with somebody who she hasn't met. Before I met Cyn, I would usually be over my mama's house twenty-four seven, but now I can't even remember the last time I was over there or even bothered to call her.

"Why are you just now telling me this after I just got done cooking a simply ass burger and some fries? She is going to think that I don't be feeding you good here."

"Cyn, will you chill the fuck out with that bullshit, please? Trust me when I tell you that food will be the last thing that's her mind. That lady is not your typical mother." When I said that, she looked at me confused.

"What do you mean by that?"

"My mama taught me everything I know when it came to drugs and being in the streets."

"Are you serious? Mama used to be a trapper?" She asked with an interested look on her face.

"I sure did, suga, how do you think Money knows how to get his hands dirty without getting caught? Trapping has always been in our blood," my mama said, walking in the kitchen with a smile on her face. Cyn quickly got up and started smiling

"Hello, I'm Cynthia..."

"Oh, girl, sit yo' ass down. I know exactly who you and your brother are."

"Really?"

"Hell yea I do. Other than Money, you and Jamal are the hottest trappers in Compton. Now when it comes to your personal lives, I have no clue how you are, and I hope you're not as ruthless to my son as you are in the streets," my mama threatened as she bent down and kissed my cheek.

"Oh no, ma'am. I make sure to separate business with pleasure. I might be a savage in the streets, but I'm a sweetheart at home, and make sure to take care of your nappy headed son here."

"How long have you two known each other?" Cyn looked at me nervously for my help. I just shook my head and chuckled because I know my mama could be intimidating.

"We have only been knowing each other for about what

three or four months now?" I looked at Cyn and she smiled while nodding her head yes.

"And y'all are already moving in with each other and damn near married? How do y'all know that y'all are the one for each other?" If my mama wasn't going to complain about anything else, I knew she was going to have something to say about Cyn and I moving way to fast, but I could honestly care less about what anybody has got to say about my relationship with the love of my life.

"With all due respect, ma'am, I really don't care what you or anybody has to say about us because we know that we do love each other genuinely no matter how long it took us to figure it out. I understand that it's kind of weird how fast we moved, but our love is unconditional and I'm not going anywhere." I know that this is not a good moment, but it made my dick hard as fuck watching Cyn defend our love to my mother. At that very moment was when I knew that she was the one because nobody has ever had the balls to stand up to my mama like that. Kash was coming out and I was feeling the fuck out of that.

"Never in my life have I witnessed anybody talk to me the way you just did, and I'm honestly happy that you are confident enough to do so. As soon as I walked in the door, I knew that you were the one for my son just by looking at you. I really don't care how long y'all knew each other because his father and I were just like y'all."

"Really?" I asked, surprised.

"Hell yea we were. When I met your father, we dated the first day, fell in love the second day, and by the time the third day came, we were married. Falling in love fast with the right person is in your blood, son, and I know that she is the right one?"

"How?" Jamal asked.

"Because she has that powerful demeanor just like my son. She is going to be right by his side through thick and thin just like I was with my husband. He's the reason why I'm so grimy and hard right now. Baby, that killer instinct that you I know you have inside of you, let her out because I will tell you right now, there is no better feeling than fighting and killing for the man you love." Cyn was looking at me with a smile on her face the whole time my mama was talking. There is no doubt in my mind when it comes to Cyn that she is the one for me, because she is. Cyn has brought so much joy in my life, and I can't wait to call her my wife soon.

"Don't be boosting her head up, ma; it's already too big," I joked, which caused her to laugh.

"Don't be talking about me like that, negro; you're the reason why my head is so big right now. Nikki and I are about to go shopping, do you want to go, Mrs. Walker?"

"If you don't mind hanging out with little ole me. I have been wanting to go to the mall for the longest but I only hang out with men and they hate going shopping with me."

"That's 'cause you like to spend an hour in one store ma," I replied, speaking for all of my mother friends. My mama is such a gangster females tend to be intimidated by her, so she has no girlfriends.

"Of course I want to hang out with you, let me go upstairs so I can get dressed and I will be back down." Cyn hopped her happy ass upstairs to go put something on leaving my mama in there with me and Jamal. I just hope that she doesn't turn into one of them mothers who talks about their child's significant other when they walk out the room.

"You better watch out, Terran, you got your hands full with that one," my mama said as she touched my shoulder.

"What do you mean I have my hands full?"

"That girl is going to give you a run for your money. I can see that now. Not only is she a handful when it comes to your personal life, she is going to be too much to handle in the streets as well. Didn't you tell me that she is going to be a part of all of your businesses now?" I nodded my head yes instead of responding.

"She was already badass when it came to being the streets, and now that you are teaching her how to be the connect and helping her learn what you do on a daily basis, she is going to give you a run for your money."

"I'm already knowing that, mama."

"You, Cyn, and Jamal are going to be the most powerful people in the state of Cali, and y'all need to learn how to control that power. Y'all are going to have a lot of jealous people out here that is going to try and take everything that all of you worked hard for, but you have to learn how to be smart about handling this bullshit. Certain situations doesn't have to be solved by killing people, all it takes is just one conversation." Jamal and I both nodded our heads understanding where she was coming from. My mama usually doesn't get in to my business only when it's necessary.

"Thanks for dropping knowledge on us, ma. I felt like we really needed that talk to get us motivated."

"I'm ready," Cyn stated, walking back in the kitchen with Nikki behind her. My mama kissed my cheek and walked out the kitchen.

"Are you taking my car?" I asked Cyn, while standing up and pulling her towards me.

"Only if you want me to."

"Yea go ahead, and call me when y'all made it there."

"Okay, I love you."

"I love you too, baby." I kissed her sweet lips and watched as they walked out the door. I'm glad that her and my mother was getting along, but I am also worried that they are going to get close enough and start double teaming me.

"Well, since the women bailed on us, do you want to go ahead and get this meeting out the way with Teddy?"

"We might as well; I do want to stop by Derrick's house first." Jamal gave me the side eye probably trying to figure out where my head was at.

"Want me to go with you?"

"Are you going to be able to be in the same room as him without losing yo' cool?"

"Yea." Was all he said before walking out the kitchen. I already knew that his ass was lying, but I couldn't control a grown man and his feelings. I just hope and pray that Jamal doesn't kill my brother.

. . . .

"Look, I did not come here to start anything or kill anybody so will you please try to be on your best behavior, man?" Jamal looked at me for a minute before bursting out laughing.

"Ain't nobody worried about that nigga, man, I'm just here for moral support. Come on so we can get on to bigger and better things." I got out the car and starting walking to Derrick's home.

"What the fuck are you doing here, Terran?" Derrick asked as soon as he saw me walk in to his house. I looked at him long and hard trying to keep my composure. The whole ride over here I didn't know how I was going to react, but now that I am here, I want to end his life right now. I have to fight that urge.

"I just came over here to talk to you to see where yo' head is at right now, bro, that's it."

"So why did you bring yo' bodyguard?" He asked, referring to Jamal. I'm so glad that he is a very patient person, and it takes a lot for him to get mad 'cause he didn't do anything but laugh and sat down besides Derrick.

"You are one silly son of a bitch, you know that? I'm just here to make sure that he doesn't kill you, so you might want to leave me the fuck alone." Derrick looked at me for a long time before sighing and issuing me to have a seat.

"So what did you want to talk about, Terran?"

"I'm just trying to figure out why you thought it would be a good idea to team up with Gritt to try to kill me and Jamal over here?"

"Oh and don't forget about my sister, bro?" Jamal said, adding his two cents and causing Derrick to get uncomfortable.

"Do we really have to talk about that right now in front

of him, man?" Derrick asked, while looking me directly in the eyes.

"No offense, bro, but Jamal has every right to be in here with us."

"Man, I just didn't like the way you have been acting."

"What do you mean?" I asked, confused.

"Ever since you linked up with him and started fucking his sister, you have been acting shady as fuck, and barely come around. That shit was pissing me off."

"First of, I'm not fucking Cyn, I am in a relationship with her, and we both decided that it would be a smart move to get in business with Jamal, so why are you deciding to change your mind?"

"Because you started acting different with me, and you was too busy with Cyn and trying to build a friendship with Jamal, you forgot about me and moms." I really didn't believe Nikki when she said that Derrick was jealous of my relationship with Cyn, but I'm actually noticing that he is jealous of my relationship with her and Jamal and to me that's childish as fuck.

"Are you being serious right now, Derrick? We are twenty-three years old and you're still acting childish. I can't believe that you're actually jealous of a grown ass man and my relationship with my woman!"

"Man, you have to understand where I'm coming from right now. It has always been you and I since we were little, and all of a sudden things changed when Jamal and Cyn comes in the picture."

"So you're mad that you have to share his attention with other people?" Jamal asked.

"Come on, man. Now is not the time for jokes," I replied, trying to get him to chill out before I lose my mind.

"Man, I'm not being funny, I'm being serious as fuck right now. Some people don't know how to act when they have to share a person who has been by there side since day one. Not having all of their attention can cause them to go crazy. That's probably what happened in this case." When he started explaining what he meant, it actually made sense.

"Is that how you felt, bro?" Derrick sighed and nodded his head.

"If that was the case, you should have just talked to me instead of going behind my back trying to help Gritt kill me. Do you understand what you just did, bro? I can't trust yo' ass, and I really don't want to be around you."

"I understand that, bro and I apologize for that, but how are not going to be around me when we work together?" He asked, confused. I looked at Jamal letting him know that he could tell him.

"Well, I'm sorry to tell you this, but your assistance will no longer be needed in the business. Terran and I have decided that it would be best if we replace you with somebody who is more trustworthy and who we could depend on. As of now, you are not allowed in any of the traps, offices, meetings, or re-up locations. If somebody sees you at any of those places, we will have to kill you, unfortunately. We also need you to sign this contract stating that if for some reason Kash's or Money's identity gets revealed, you will be held reasonable and the only consequence for that is torture and death. If you refuse to sign it right now, then we have no choice but to kill you right now," Jamal quickly said with a smile on his face like he was enjoying every minute of it. I looked at Derrick and you can tell that he was devastated because that was his only income at the moment.

"Are you being serious right now, bro? All because of a fucking mistake?"

"If you think that what you did was only a mistake then something must really be wrong with you, my nigga. I told you from the jump how dirty Gritt was and how you needed to stay away from him because he's not trustworthy, but you decided to say fuck yo' best friend and help him kill me! So yes, I'm being serious right now, and I'm sorry that it has to come to this but it is what it is, now like Jamal said, we are going to need you to sign this paper." He chuckled then snatched the paper from Jamal and signed it.

"There and don't worry, I'm not going to tell nobody anything. You can trust me with that information because my life is more important, now will y'all please get the fuck out my house so I can look for a fucking job?" I stood there for a minute debating on if I wanted to ask Jamal if he could let him work at the car shop, but I already knew that he was going to say no.

"Look, bro, I usually don't do this to people who tried to drug my girl and kill me and my sis, but I know how much this nigga over here care about you... no gay shit, but if I see that you are not on any bullshit for at least a month then I will give you a job at my shop, but you cannot be hanging out with Gritt's ass." Derrick smirked and nodded his head.

"You got my word man, thank you." Jamal nodded his head and walked out the door. I held my hand out for Derrick to shake just to let him know that I still kind of respect him.

Once I was back outside in the car, I pulled out my phone and texted Cyn.

ME: YOU BETTER NOT BE GIVING MY MAMA A HARD TIME.

Queen: Negro please. Yo' mama and Nikki left me like five minutes ago to go to the food court.

ME: WELL WYD?

QUEEN: GETTING YOU A GIFT.

ME: LET ME SEE

"Aye bro, are you driving, or do you want me to?" Jamal asked, interrupting my thoughts. I was getting ready to respond, but Cyn threw me off by sending me a picture of her in some sexy ass red lingerie that instantly made me brick up.

Me: Yo' ass better be at home with that same energy 'cause I'm fucking you silly.

QUEEN: WE WILL BE WAITING ON YOU, DADDY

She sent me a picture of her kitty which made me want to put this meeting on pause so I can go home to my wife and damage her insides.

"Bro, you and Cyn and sext later, I need to know if you want me to drive or not," Jamal yelled, pissing me off.

"Yea you're driving, and don't be mad just because you ain't getting no pussy from yo' bitch, my nigga."

"This nigga better not be on no bullshit right now," Jamal mumbled, sounding pissed. I looked up from my phone and noticed Gritt sitting on the steps looking lost.

"How in the fuck did he know we was coming here?" I asked, confused.

"He didn't, one of our workers called me like two days ago saying that he has been sitting in the same spot not talking to anybody," Jamal explained, while parking the car and getting out. I don't know why he was worried about Derrick when his own cousin is who we have to worry about.

"What the fuck is going on with you, Gritt? Didn't I tell yo ass that I don't want to see you again?" Jamal yelled. Gritt looked at him with gloomy eyes. It actually looked like something was wrong with him.

"Do you think I actually want to be here just so you can talk bad to me Jamal? Yea I know that I fucked up this time and I am lucky to be alive, but I need your help although I don't deserve it."

"Help with what?"

"Can we talk about it inside, man please? I promised I'm not on any bullshit, I just need your help." Jamal looked at me and I just shrugged. For some reason, I feel like he is being genuine, especially for him to be sitting on these stairs for days not knowing if Jamal was going to show up.

"Look, man, I'm busy right now but go home take a shower, change clothes, and meet me at the house. If you try anything, I promise I won't hesitate to put a bullet in yo' ass." Gritt nodded his head and walked away.

"Do you think he's up to something?" Jamal asked me, probably trying to see if he was making the right decision.

"I don't think so surprisingly. You could tell by his demeanor that something was really going on with him. I think you should talk to him just to see what's going on, and if he really needs your help, but if you think that he is on bullshit then just say the word, and I will get rid of him."

"Are y'all talking about Gritt?" Teddy asked as soon as we walked in to the office.

"Yea, has he came in here for anything, and how long has yo' ass been in here?" Jamal asked.

"Shit for like an hour now, and yea when he saw me pulling in, he waited for like thirty minutes before coming and asking me if he could hide out in here until you came. I told his ass no and he needs to leave before I shoot his ass." I sat down in the seat closest to the door and just listened to what Teddy was saying. It sounded like he has always had Jamal's back, and he is not going to turn on him.

"I told him to just meet me at my house, so I can see what this nigga is up to."

"Hopefully he's not on any bullshit, man." I made known as I placed my gun on the table.

"So why did y'all pull me away from working if you don't mind me asking?"

"We actually needed to talk to you about your position in

the business," Jamal answered, while looking at me waiting for me to finish.

"Y'all got me fucked up if y'all think I'm about to just let y'all take my job away from me. I'll die before I just walk away that easy, and I haven't even did anything to get my job taken away from me." He pulled out his gun and aimed it at us ready for war. That's when I knew that he was right for this position. Any man that's willing to kill anybody just to prove their loyalty to the game is somebody that I want working with me.

"Damn nigga, chill yo' hostile ass out. Ain't nobody trying to take your job away from you, we just wanted to give you the promotion that you deserve." He looked at me for a moment before smiling.

"My bad, nigga. I really thought I was going to have to kill y'all niggas, but if I accept this promotion will I still be handling the finances, and the traps?"

"Well, you will be taking Derrick's spot as my right hand and we was going to replace you with somebody else, but if you want to get those positions then go for it."

"Yea I will because I don't trust nobody else when it comes to handling the money no offense."

"None taken, bro. I will be announcing your promotion today at the meeting."

"So will I be able to meet Kash and Money?" He asked, which cause me to smirk.

"Yes, but before you will be able to meet them, you have to sign a contract to keep their identity a secret, and if for some reason their identity comes out, we will have no choice but to end your life." He nodded his head in understanding while I handed him the contract.

"Y'all don't have to worry about me telling a soul. Jamal is like a brother to him and I wouldn't do anything to jeopardize our friendship."

"After the meeting today you need to stay a little while longer so you can meet Kash and Money."

"Wait… So Money is going to be at the meeting today?" He

asked, shocked.

"You know Money don't do re-up meetings, man. He will be there, just not in the meeting."

"Ah-ight man, I will see y'all at the meeting later on." We all slapped hands and walked out at the same time. I feel like Jamal and I made the right decision by giving Teddy the job, I just hope that he does not make me regret the choice that I made.

CHAPTER 8

CYN

"Gritt, what are you doing here?" I was at my brother's apartment waiting for them to come get me when Gritt walked in the door. I haven't seen him since we found out that he was trying to kill us, so I didn't know how to deal with him being here. I quickly grabbed the gun from my brother's closet and sat it on the table just in case he is on some bullshit.

"Jamal told me to come and wait on him here. I don't want any trouble, Cyn; I just needed y'all help." I gave him a strange look, trying to see if he was telling the truth or not.

"What do you need help with, Gritt?"

"I fucked up, Cyn." He placed his hands on his head and plopped down on the couch.

"Fucked up how?"

"I stole from some niggas that Jamal used to have beef with a long time ago, and I think that they are after him now."

"What the fuck you mean, Gritt? Please tell me that you are not that stupid to fuck with the same niggas that he had a problem with?"

"I know I fucked up, Cyn, but I need y'all help, man. They are going to kill me once they find out where I'm at." I looked at him like he was dumb. I honestly could care less about how he was feeling at the moment.

"Do you think I give a fuck about them killing you, Gritt? You stole from some niggas that have been waiting for a reason to come after my brother, and you think I give a fuck about you? You better hope and pray that Jamal does not kill you before he gets information from you, because you really fucked up this time."

"What are y'all in here talking about, and how did you get

in my house, Cyn?" Jamal asked, while walking in. It looked like him and Terran was in a good mood, so let's hope that it stays that way.

"What's going on, baby?" Terran said, slapping my ass. I stood on my tippy toes and kissed his soft lips.

"You will see in a minute, go ahead and tell them what you need help with, Gregory," I said, sitting down so I could enjoy the show. Terran walked away from and stood next to Jamal.

"What's going on, Gritt? What have you gotten yourself into now?" Jamal asked.

"I fucked up and robbed Juice and his crew." When he said that, both Terran and Jamal started pacing back and forth. I'm pretty sure that they wasn't scared, they just didn't want any more problems with Juice and his peoples. Juice used to work with Teddy and my brother back when they were just corner boys, but when Juice started getting greedy, Teddy and Jamal decided to do things on their own which caused Juice to get mad and set them up. Their little feud went on for about four months until they all decided to just end the war and stay out of each other's way, well until now.

"Why in the fuck would you even think that it's okay to even be in Juice's hood, man!" Jamal yelled.

"Man, I wasn't thinking straight. I didn't know that they were going to come for you because of my fuck up."

"What do you mean come for me, man?"

"Some niggas rolled up to my crib telling me that they knew that you and Money teamed up and how I fucked up by stealing from them. He told me to tell you that Juice has been waiting on this day for the longest." Terran sat down on the couch and laughed, looking all good and shit.

"Nigga, do you realize what you just did? I even had a problem with Juice, and I know for a fact that his ass plays dirty as fuck. You done started some shit that we had nothing to do with."

"His ass just stared and unnecessary war with this nigga.

You might wanna get the fuck out my face before I put a bullet in yours, and you better not even try running because I will find yo' dumb ass." Gritt held his head down and just walked out the door without saying anything back which was a smart idea. I think he knows that he fucked up this time, and this just might end his life.

"I can't believe that this nigga thought it would be a good idea to steal from Juice ass. What would make him do some stupid ass shit like that?" Jamal asked, trying to keep calm.

"His ass wasn't thinking at all, but you know that I'm down with whatever you want to do." Terran let it be known.

"Knowing Juice, all you have to do is throw a couple of bands at him and he will go back in to hiding along with his crew," I told Jamal.

"Terran and I will go and try to talk to him probably tomorrow or something, but I want you to stay away from him." I tilted my head to the side and just stared at him trying to figure out if I should be offended or not.

"You don't think I can handle Juice?"

"Nah, I don't." Terran couldn't do anything but laugh because he knew that I was about to make a lie out of Jamal. I just smirked and sat back without saying anything to him.

"Come on, bro, you know damn well Kash can handle Juice's pussy ass. You better stop underestimating and treating Cyn like she's a kid. You know I would have never trusted her with my shit if I thought that she wasn't made for it." Jamal looked at me for a minute before mugging the fuck out of me.

"I just don't want to think of my little sister as being a ruthless killer like yo' ass."

"Well, you better start thinking that because her ass might be worse than me. Come on so we can get this meeting over with." Terran yanked me up from my seat and pulled me towards him.

"You got that lingerie, right?" He whispered in my ear.

"You know I did, daddy."

"Well, let's get this over with, so I can beat that pussy up.

Oh and you know I'm gone let you go after Juice so you can prove yo' brother wrong, right?"

"I was already ahead of you, baby. It's time that Kash starts making her mark in these streets.

• •

"Before everybody leaves, I need you to double check and make sure that your product is correct and you have the exact same amount as you did at the last re-up," I announced from behind the screen. The meeting went better and smoother than I thought. Everyone treated me with respect and didn't try to play me because I was a woman. Even though I was behind a screen, I knew that my power invaded the room.

"Oh, and before I let y'all go, I have something to announce," Jamal mentioned, getting out of his seat and walking to the front of the room with Terran right behind him.

"What's going on, boss?" One of the workers asked.

"As you all know and can see, we had to let Derrick go because he wasn't loyal to the team. After that happened I sat down and had a nice, long talk with Terran, Kash, and Money so we can discuss who we want to replace him with. We decided that we wanted it to be somebody who has been by my side fighting the same battle as me since day one. Somebody who has not only showed his loyalty to me, but to the whole team and who has also gave their all to this business. The only person who I trust with everyone's life is Teddy," Terran said, giving this long and dramatic speech.

"It's about damn time!" Everyone shouted while clapping their hands.

"Not only will Teddy be the lead, but he will also still be in charge of the finance and the traps. Is everyone coo with that?" They all nodded their heads without saying anything.

"Kash, is that all you needed?" Jamal asked, looking at the screen.

"Yes, that's all I needed. Oh, one more thing, the trap that Gritt was in charge of keeps coming up short, and I need that to be fixed as soon as possible. Money and I will be doing random pop ups at the traps tomorrow, and if we see shit we don't like, then there will be consequences. If nobody has any questions or concerns, then you are dismissed." Once everybody was out of the office, we waited about ten minutes before we started talking.

"Okay Teddy, so before Money and I agree to showing you who we really are, I just need to make sure that you are really loyal to this team. We are very picky and strict on who we want to know about us, and even though I have a strong feeling that you're not going to fuck us over, I just need for you to tell me why you deserve to see us," I demanded.

"Well, first of all, I just want to let the both of you know that it's an honor to even be in the same room as you, and I appreciate this opportunity. I also want to let you know that even though you guys haven't known me for a long time like Jamal have, not to be cocky, but I feel like I have proven my loyalty to this family, and team since I have known them. There is no disloyalty in my blood, and there will never be." I smiled, stood up from my seat, and walked from being the door. When Teddy saw me standing there, he looked at me confused before laughing.

"You have got to be shitting me, man, so you're Kash?" Teddy said, laughing.

"In the flesh."

"So that means that yo' ass has been Money this whole time. Damn, I would have never guessed this shit a day in my life."

"Well, bro, now you know," Terran said.

"Now that I know it's y'all, I definitely won't say shit, 'cause I know how y'all get down. I'm even gone try to forget that I know who it is." We all stood around and just laughed. I don't think that we have to worry about Teddy fat ass telling a soul.

"I'm about to get out of here because this drug shit makes me itch," I complained.

"Well, you better get used to scratching, because this is

your life now baby girl. Now let's go so I can put a baby in yo' sister.," Terran somewhat joked, while putting me in a bear hug.

"I almost shot yo bitch ass, my nigga. My sister can't get pregnant because she's a fucking virgin, ain't that right, Cynthia?"

"Mhmmm sure," I mumbled, walking out the door in a fast pace trying to get away from my brother before he kills me.

"You know yo' brother is going to beat yo' ass the next time he sees you, right?" Terran asked as he got in the car and drove off.

"Ain't nobody tripping off Jamal's sensitive ass. Anyways, I wanted to talk to you about something just so I can see where yo' mind is at."

"What's going on, baby?"

"Do you actually believe what Gritt said?" He was quiet for a minute before he started to chuckle.

"You don't believe him?"

"Hell nah, I don't! Gritt has tried this bullshit before, and he ended up fucking us over in the end. He might have looked like he was being serious, but I know my cousin."

"So what are you saying exactly?"

"Either he's working with Juice, and they have a plan to come after us, or he's trying to set us up so that we can go after him and start a war, but either way it goes he is up to something."

"Why do you think it's Gritt and not Juice?"

"Juice might be a dirty ass nigga, but what he won't do is come after people who he knows is going kill him and his crew. Juice has always been a scary ass nigga when it came to Jamal and Teddy, so I know for a fact that his ass didn't send nobody over to Gritt's house just to threaten y'all. I smell some bullshit," I admitted. I honestly don't think that we have to worry about Juice because he ain't dumb enough to start a war with us on purpose when he knows that Jamal and Money are working together now.

"Now that you mention it, that shit Gritt said don't make

sense at all. So do you want to tell Jamal, or do you want to handle it?"

"I really feel like I should handle it since Jamal is doubting me and shit. I think I need to show him that his little sister has more juice than he think I have."

"So, when are you going to go pay Juice a visit?"

"Probably sometime tomorrow, I really just want to go home and spend time with you tonight." I leaned over and kissed his sweet lips. I have never been this happy with a guy a day in my life. Terran has opened my eyes and made me realize that I need to stop trying to change men to be the perfect man for me and maybe it's me who needs to change. I know that I've lived in the hood of Compton and killed a couple of people, but I would have never thought that I would actually be a Queen Pin. I guess that's what I get for trying to act like I'm better than them.

By the time we made it home, the both of us was tired from being out the house all day, so we just ordered Chinese food and cuddled in the bed together.

"I don't mean to get all serious and shit, but did you think that we would actually be this deep in a relationship already?" Terran asked out of the blue.

"I really didn't, and it's crazy because I never did anything like this before."

"What do you mean?"

"Well, I usually take things a lot slower with men, and I usually don't date guys who are in the streets, but you were different," I revealed, having him look at me strangely.

"What do you mean I was different? I hope that was meant in a good way."

"Of course it is, baby. When I first met you, it felt like I've known you my whole life which was strange. It was like I trusted and fell in love with you instantly. It usually takes me at least two months for me to even go out with a guy, but I moved in with you literally the next month," I confessed as I shoved a fork full of noodles in my mouth.

"That's crazy because I felt the same way, but the only difference between us is I have a problem with fallen in love with the wrong women."

"What the fuck do you mean by that?" I asked, getting slightly offended.

"I didn't mean you, crazy. I'm just saying that every woman who I decided to give a chance to always made me regret it. They were either only with me for the money, dick, or both. None of the love that they gave me was genuine, but with you, I know it is. I don't know what it was about you, but I just knew that you were the one for me." I looked at him and blushed. This man is perfect for me.

"Let's go and get married," I blurted out which caused him to choke on his food.

"Are you serious, Cyn?"

"Dead ass, baby. We already know that we are not going anywhere, and I'm ready to be your wife, so let's go get married right now."

"So what are we going to do, go to Vegas?"

"Hell yea. Look I don't need no big extravagant wedding. As long as I am able to call you my husband, I'm fine."

"Well shit, pack an overnight bag and let's go! You already know that I'm down with making you my wife. What about the rings though? All of the jewelry stores are closed."

"We can get rings tomorrow; it takes about an hour to get there by plane so I can see if that have some last-minute plane tickets."

"I have a private jet, baby," Terran said.

"Well, let's go!" I yelled excitedly while jumping on the bed. I can believe that I was about to marry the love of my life.

THE NEXT DAY

"How are you feeling, Mrs. Walker?" Terran asked with a huge smile on his face as we walked hand in hand out of the jewelry store.

"Like I'm the luckiest women in the world." I blushed, wrapping my arms around his neck when we made it to the car. As soon as we made it to Vegas, we wasted no time getting married. I already know that I'm going to get an earful from my parents and Jamal, but I don't even care because they all love Terran, and they simply can't tell me what the fuck to do with my life.

"Well, let's go home so I can fuck my wife." He winked and helped me in the car never taking his beautiful eyes off me. I pulled out my ringing phone and answered.

"Hey, best friend!" I shouted when I heard Nikki's voice.

"Bitch, don't hey best friend me. Where the fuck are you at Cyn? Jamal and I have been blowing up both of y'all phones and y'all haven't been answering. On top of that y'all haven't been at home, so you better have a good fucking reason as to why y'all have been ignoring us." I laughed and looked at Terran to see if he wanted me to tell them.

"Go ahead, baby," he whispered.

"Are you with Jamal now, Nikki?"

"Bitch, you know I am."

"Well, put me on speaker." It was quiet for about ten seconds before I heard his voice.

"You better not be on no bullshit, Cyn. Where are y'all motherfuckas at?"

"Vegas," I simply said.

"Why in the fuck.... Tell me y'all didn't just do what I

think y'all did," Jamal said, sounding happy but mad at the same time.

"Yep, we got married last night!" I shouted!

"YASSS BITCH!!!!! I told Jamal that's what was probably going on, but he didn't want to believe me. I don't know about him, but I'm happy for you, best friend! Bih done found her a man and don't know how to act." I could tell that Nikki's over-dramatic ass was doing something crazy and I couldn't do nothing but laugh.

"You good over there, bro?" Terran asked, trying to get Jamal's attention.

"I should beat the both of y'all ass for sneaking away and not telling nobody, but I'm happy for y'all."

"Thank you, Mal! We are on our way back so we will probably stop by and chill for a minute. I love y'all!"

"We love you too," Nikki said then hung up the phone. I am so glad that they are not mad about us not telling them that we are getting married, but now I have to worry about my parents.

"Do you just want to go straight to Juice?" He asked, stirring me out of my thoughts.

"Do you know where he be at during the day?"

"You know I do, baby. Money knows everything about everybody."

"Well, let's go then." It took us about three hours to get home, change clothes and go to one of Juice's spot.

"Do you think that we are going to have a problem with him today?" Terran questioned, while putting his gun on his waist.

"I highly doubt it, but we will see." When we got out the car, all of his workers stopped doing what they were doing and pulled out their guns, aiming at us. They were probably intimidated because we were dressed in all black with a black mask on.

"We are not here to start trouble; we just need to talk to Juice," Terran stated.

"And who are y'all supposed to be?"

"I'm Kash and this is Money, now can you please tell your boss that we need to see him before things get ugly around here." Now knowing who we were, they nodded their heads and quickly walked in the house scared for their lives.

"I just love seeing how much effect I have on niggas," I whispered to Terran.

"He said come in," one of his workers said, walking us in. When we made it in the house, Juice was sitting on the couch playing the game like he doesn't have a care in the world. That lets me know that he is sloppy when it comes to his business.

"What can I do for you two?" He asked, never taking his eyes off the tv which pissed me off. I pulled out my gun and shot the tv.

"When we are in your presence then you need to pay attention to us. That's the first sign of respect." He looked at me and started laughing.

"And who are you supposed to be? Money's little guard dog?" Money chuckled and just sat down.

"You know you just fucked up, man? Kash does not like to be disrespected," Money said.

"You think I give a fuck about respecting her when she just came in and started tripping. I don't give a fuck how powerful the both of y'all claim y'all are, you are in my part of town, so you better watch what you say," he threatened, which pissed me off.

"I came here with a calm and positive vibe, but you just fucked it up for yourself so let me tell you how this visit is going to go. You are going to tell us what we need to know and you will live to see another day, but if you feel like you want to go another route and get killed, then you go ahead. The ball is in your court, my nigga." I guess he figured out that I was not playing because he took one last pull from the blunt he was smoking and just looked at us.

"What the fuck are y'all here for?"

"Gritt came to Money and Jamal saying that one of your

workers came to his house threating Jamal and I just need to make sure that it was telling the truth." Juice looked at me confused.

"What are you talking about, Kash? I did send one of my workers over there, but it was not to threaten Jamal. Gritt was trying to get put on with my crew and when I told him no because I knew how he got down, him and one of his friends robbed one of my corner boys. So I had one of my workers stop by his house and tell him that he has two days to come up with my shit or we are going to kill him. Jamal don't have anything to do with this."

I looked at Money with an 'I told you so' look. I knew that Juice wouldn't do no shit that bold ever, but what I do know is that my cousin knows how to lie his ass off when he wants the heat to be taken off him.

"So everything that Gritt said was a lie basically?"

"Man, hell yea it's a lie. I don't fuck with Jamal, or Money like that but I also know that I don't want to start no war and shit with them. I ain't no bitch, but I know how to pick and choose my battles. I'm not worried about y'all or Jamal, but Gritt is who y'all need to be worried about."

"What do you mean?" I asked.

"I think that Gritt is going around trying to start some shit with people who he know y'all don't fuck with because he is scared of doing something himself. I'll make sure to keep my eyes and ears on the streets and let y'all know if I see something suspicious."

"Good looking out, man and my bad about the tv, Kash just don't like to be disrespected," Money said, while laughing and getting up out his seat.

"What the fuck are you apologizing for? I would do that shit again if I feel threatened."

"I'm not tripping off it, Money. If she's anything like you, then Compton needs to watch out." I laughed and just walked out the door. Juice might not have anything to do with what Gritt is talking about, but I still don't trust his ass. When I made it outside, I saw the same car that passed us when we first got here ride past again which was never a good sign.

"What's wrong, baby?" Money asked, placing his hand on my back.

"That's the same car that passed us when we first got here. Juice, do you have a problem with anybody?" I asked, while looking back. Juice was standing in the doorway with his gun already in his hand.

"I was about to ask y'all the same damn thing; it's been quiet as fuck over here for a while."

"Same with us. If that car ride past one more time, I'm just gone start bussin'," I said, letting it be known. Just like I expected, I saw the car slowing riding past while letting their window down but I didn't give them time to even pull out their gun because I started letting off rounds. Money was by my side busting his gun as well and it was a sexy ass sight. Whoever it was must have had a problem with us because not once did they aim their gun at Juice, but he was shooting at them right along with us.

"Them niggas ain't letting up.! Money yelled.

"Let's end this shit then daddy." We both started walking up to the car like we were bulletproof and started offing niggas left and right. The only person who was left breathing was the driver. Money ran over to the driver side and pulled him out the car.

"Call Jamal and tell him to meet us at the warehouse," Money demanded which made my pussy wet. I bit my bottom lip, nodded my head and pulled out my phone.

"What's up, sis?"

"Meet us at the warehouse like now."

"I'm on my way," he said then hung up. That's one thing that I love about my brother when it comes to handling business. He never asks questions about what's going on, he will just do what he has to do to protect me and his business.

"I don't know if this has anything to do with us, but if it did, I apologize and I will pay for any damages," I said, walking up to Juice.

"It's coo, man; I'm not tripping off this shit. I just called the cleanup crew so they should be here in a minute. I'm going with y'all to the warehouse." I looked at him like he was crazy.

"If Jamal and Teddy see you walking in with us, they are going to flip."

"Man, I'm not tripping of those niggas Kash. Plus,, I think I can help if I have any information on anything."

"Let me check with Money." He nodded his head and I walked away.

"What was y'all over there talking about?"

"He wants to go with us to the warehouse, but I told him that I will check with you because I didn't know how Jamal or Teddy would feel about it."

"Tell him to come on, I will handle Jamal and Teddy. I feel like we are going to need him anyways, and plus he is acting like he got some sense now." I nodded at Juice to let him know that it was okay for him to go and he nodded back and walked to the car. I hope my brothers don't lose it when they see us walking in with Juice.

• •

"Please tell me you brought this nigga here so we could kill him," Jamal said as soon as he saw us walk in with Juice.

"Actually, he's here to help us," I said in a matter of fact tone.

"Help? You must be out of yo' motherfuckin' mind, Kash! What could this nigga possibly help us with when he is trying to kill me?"

"If you would listen to me instead of overtalking me then I can explain."

"What the fuck is going on, Kash?" Teddy asked in a calm manner.

"The shit that Gritt told us was bullshit! Juice told us that he did send one of his workers to Gritt's house, but it was not to threaten you or Money. Gritt was trying to get put on with his crew, probably because we wouldn't let him on ours, but when Juice told him no because he knew how he got down, Gritt and one of his friends robbed one of Juice's corner boys. So he had one of his workers stop by his house and tell him that he has two days to come up with his shit or he is going to kill him. We weren't even brought up in the conversation."

Jamal and Teddy both looked at each other contemplating on what to do next. They grew up with Juice so they would know if he's bullshitting or not.

"So why are you here, my nigga?" Jamal asked.

"Because I just wanted you to hear from me that I don't have a problem with y'all anymore. That shit that happened was in the past and I'm not dwelling on the past anymore. I also thought I could help with the situation."

"What situation?" Teddy and Jamal both asked at the same time. Money walked out to go get ole dude. He threw him down on the grown and stood beside Jamal.

"Can somebody explain to us what's going on please?" Teddy asked, getting irritated.

"Long story short, when we were about to leave Juice's trap, a car kept riding past, so I got suspicious. I pulled my gun out, and we were all in the middle of a fucking shootout, but the thing is they weren't aiming at Juice. They were aiming and Money and I."

"Damn, Kash, who have you pissed off already?" Teddy joked.

"So who is this dude?" Jamal asked, pointing at the guy who looked scared for his life.

"He was the driver, and before y'all ask, Juice was helping us out a lot."

"Good looking out," Jamal said, which caused me to smile.

"No problem, man, but can I know who Kash and Money are? This shit is fucking with me," Juice laughed, which cause me to chuckle. I guess we were doing a hell of a good job at hiding our identities.

"Nah, we don't trust you like that, man. Who are you

working for, my nigga?" Money asked, walking up to the guy and snatching the tape off of his mouth.

"I'm not telling you shit." Money and I both chuckled at the same time.

"Let me let you in on a little secret, my dude. These niggas here don't have any patience when it comes to this kind of shit, so they would probably just kill yo' ass instantly, but my wife and I love torturing niggas, and we have all night. The choice is yours." Money shrugged and pulled a chair in from of him. I walked over to him and sat on his lap.

"Who are you working for, and how did you know that we were going to be with Juice?" He just looked at me and started laughing.

"Do yo' thing, baby," Money whispered in my ear. I got up and walked over to the cabinet to get a knife and some salt.

"W-what are you about to do with that?" The guy asked, stuttering.

"I'm about to cook steak. What the fuck do you think I'm about to do with this shit? Now I'm going to ask you one last time, and if I feel like you are going to be on bullshit, then I'm going to start slicing. Who are you working with?" Since he took too long to answer, I walked over to him and sliced his chest open, then poured salt all in the wound.

"Ahhh shit!" He screamed out in pain.

"I liked the way yo' sexy ass just did that, Kash. Do it again," Money said, hyping me up. Just as I was about to cut him again, he spoke up.

"Gritt and Derrick gave me ten thousand dollars, to follow y'all around. They told me about how they are going to get y'all and Juice to start a war with each other so that can distract y'all from what they planned on doing. I wasn't going to do it at first because I never wanted to get on y'all bad side, but when they gave me all of that money, I had to take it because I was about to get evicted."

"What did they plan on doing?" I asked.

"Taking all of the money and product from the traps that

they was in charge over and starting their own business."

"I told you that Gritt was smartedr than he seemed to be," Juice said.

"So how did you know where Money and I was?"

"I have been sitting outside of Juice's trap ever since yesterday. Gritt told me as soon as I saw Terran or Jamal at Juice's house, call him. I didn't think that he expected for you two to personally go to Juice's house."

"Did he say anything about Cyn or Terran?" Money asked, trying to see if he knew if we were the same people.

"He said that he was going to personally handle them two, especially Cyn, but once I told him that Kash and Money, were the ones at Juice's house, he said that was even better, because that means that Terran won't have his guard dog to protect him anymore." I just laughed at how stupid Gritt was. I thought that he would have put two and two together by now and figured out who Terran and I was really Money in Kash, but I guess he didn't. In one quick motion, I pulled out my gun and shot him in the face instantly killing him.

"That nigga Gritt has to be the dumbest nigga alive," Jamal said, while chuckling.

"So what are we going to do now?" Teddy asked.

"Teddy, Juice and I needs to talk about some shit before we even think about working together again. We will let Gritt and Derrick think they did something for the rest of the day, but we are ending their lives tomorrow," Jamal said, looking pissed off.

"That sounds good to me," I replied.

"Good, come take a ride with us, Juice. Oh, and you two are meant for each because y'all are some nasty ass lunatics."

"Can you stop doubting me now?" Jamal looked back at me and smirked. I pulled out my phone and called the cleanup crew to come and take care of this situation.

"So now that our day took a turn quick, what do you want to do now?" Terran questioned as we walked out the warehouse.

"Well, first I want to get out of these dark clothes, take a shower, and fuck my husband."

"Yo' ass ain't said nothing but a word, come on." He kissed my lips and helped me in the car. I was going to deal with Derrick and Gritt tomorrow, but right now my main focus is my man.

CHAPTER 9

GRITT

"I told you that the plan was going to work, man. I don't know why you doubted me in the first place," I said to Derrick, who was pacing back and forth. The fact that I actually succeeded in started a war between Juice and Jamal is a great thing. On top of that, I managed to get Kash and Money involved is a bonus for me.

"Do you know how dumb you sound right now? You think that it's a good thing about you being able to get Kash and Money involved in this bullshit?"

"You don't think so?"

"Hell nah, I don't and that's because I know how Money work. If he comes out to personally handle business, then that means that everybody is about to die if he thinks that you are involved. This is not a good fucking thing, Gritt! They are more powerful then you think." The more I sat down and thought about what he was saying, the more worried I became. I wasn't trying to start anything with Kash and Money. I just wanted to get rid of Jamal, Cyn, and Terran, but knowing that I actually got Kash and Money was something that I don't need to be worried about.

"Well, since we were able to get all the money and product from the traps, we can go in to hiding until this shit blows over."

"I guess we can do that. I was also able to get all of the money out of Terran's safes in his old condo." I looked at him with a smirk.

"I thought you said that you was trying to stay on his good side. What happened?"

"I'm pretty sure they know that we are still working together now, but how long do you think it's going to take for them to realize what's actually going on?"

"Well, when they finally kill Juice, I know for a fact that they are going to be looking for me, but by that time we should have our own team up and running."

"Do you really think this is going to work?"

"I'm positive it's going to work, bro. I know my cousins, and I know that they are not going to back down from nothing. Trust me when I tell you, we got this, but before we leave, I have to stop by my girl's crib and leave her some money for my kid."

"Nigga you got a wife and kid and didn't tell me!" Derrick yelled. Nobody knows about my girlfriend Valencia, because I didn't want to put her in danger. She knows about my family, but what she don't know is that we are literally trying to kill each other. I'm scared that if anybody finds out about her, then she is going to be dead because of the skeletons in my closet, and I don't know what I would do if something happened to her or my unborn seed.

"I didn't tell you because I don't want her to be a part of my mess. If anything happens to her, I don't know what I would do."

"Do you understand that you can't keep her or the baby safe, man. Once you piss Kash and Money off, they are going to do any and everything in their power to make you suffer." I sat down and started rolling up a blunt without a care in the world. Jamal and Terran want to walk around and act like they are the shit, but they are about to die by the hands of somebody who they tried to play.

• •

"Valencia, where are you at, baby girl?" I unlocked her door and walked in the house.

"Hey, baby, what took you so long to get here? I missed you so much." She wobbled over to me and wrapped her arms around my waist.

"I had to take care of some business. Sit down so we can

talk." She gave me a weird look before sitting down. I placed my hand on her stomach and just looked at her.

"What's wrong? Is your family okay?"

"Yes they are fine, but I'm not."

"What's going on, baby? You're scaring me."

"It's some shit that I've been doing that I'm not proud of and I don't think that I'm going to be around much longer."

"What are you talking about, Gregory?"

"I haven't been completely honest with you, and that's only so I could protect you."

"Protect me from what? Will you please stop beating around the bush and tell me what's really going on?" I took a deep breath and started talking.

"The reason why I have so much money is because I go around stealing from people and my family. My cousin is one of the biggest drug dealers in Compton and he just recently teamed up with this guy named Money. I thought that it would be a good idea to steal a lot of money from them so I could come up, but they found out, and now they are after me." She sat there for a minute before she got up and slapped the fuck out of me.

"So you're Gritt!" She said, catching me off guard.

"How in the fuck do you know who that is?"

"Nigga, everybody in the whole fucking hood is talking about how you're grimy and how you set up your own fucking family because you're jealous of some guy who is in your cousin's business now! I can't believe that I was so fucking stupid, I have to get the fuck away from you before I get killed. You can keep your money and everything in this fucking house because I don't want it. My baby and I will be fine without you." She walked out the door without even looking back. When I looked out the window, I noticed that she didn't even get in the car that I got her, she started walking on foot. As bad as I wanted to run after her, I knew I couldn't because this was for the best.

CHAPTER 10

JAMAL

I was pissed off at the fact that I was about to let Gritt's bitch ass play the fuck out of me. I can't believe that I was even dumb enough to believe that bullshit that he was telling me. It literally took my old friend for me to realize that I have been letting Gritt get away with a lot of shit, but that ends today. As soon as I see him and Derrick's bitch ass, I'm killing them.

"You can't blame yourself for not knowing, my nigga. We all know how you are when it comes to Gritt. You don't want to kill him because he's your family and you don't know how you're going to explain that shit to your family," Teddy said, trying to make me feel better.

"It's just fucking with me though. Like, how come Cyn didn't fall for his bullshit, but I did?"

"That's because Cyn ass don't trust nobody and she's mean as fuck. Gritt just knows what to do to get under yo' skin, man, but you have to stop letting him."

"Can I say something?" Juice said. I looked at him trying to figure out if I wanted to beat his ass for all of the shit that he caused in the past, or just let shit go.

"Why do you want to help us knowing all of the bullshit that we went through in the past?" I asked.

"I'm not tripping off anything that happened in the past, man. All that shit was my fault and I apologize. I should have never agreed to fuck with Gritt."

"What do you mean fuck with Gritt?" I asked, confused.

"Man, his ass was going around saying that you and Teddy were talking shit about me, and how you really didn't want me to be a part of the shit you were building. That's when he said that he had plans to come up, I didn't know it was going to be with the money that he was stealing from y'all. As soon as I figured that out, I parted ways with his ass and decided to do my own things." Teddy and I couldn't do anything but laugh at Gritt.

"His scheming ass has always had it out for us, huh? I don't know what we could have possibly done for him to want to come in between what we worked hard for," I explained.

"Right, and if you would have just came and told us what was really going on, we would have never started beefing with yo' ass, my nigga. You are like a brother to us, and I don't know about Jamal, but it killed me to see you trying to kill us," Teddy said, speaking facts.

"I know it did, and I want to apologize for that shit. I guess I was just too headstrong to admit that I was wrong. I know that it's going to take some time for y'all to forgive and trust me again. I'm not saying that we are going to be walking around holding hands and shit, but I would like to help y'all the best way I possibly can." You could tell that he was being genuine, and now that I know that Gritt was behind us falling out and wanting to kill each other I don't think that Juice will try anything slick because he's really not a bad guy.

"Man, we are not going to hold that shit against you since it's all Gritt's fault. I don't know about Teddy, but I still trust you with my life."

"I agree with Jamal, man, you're still our brother, and we fucks with you the long way man." We all got up and gave each other a brotherly hug.

"So what's been going on with y'all niggas? I see that yo' ass is still a fucking clown," Juice said, looking at me.

"Yo' ass know I ain't never going to change, but life is good man."

"Have yo' ass finally let go of that lifelong dream you been having?"

"What dream?" I asked, confused.

"The dream where Nikki is going to finally fuck with you." I shook my head and started laughing.

"Man, I guess that dream came true, cause that's my girl now."

"Damn man, her biscuit head ass finally gave yo' goofy ass a chance, huh?"

"I mean, what can I say? Everybody loves the kid," I said, while dusting off my shoulder.

"Get the fuck out of here with that bullshit, man. Anyways, why don't you come over for Sunday dinner? I'm pretty sure my parents would love to see yo' black ass anyways."

"That sounds good to me, what about yo' fine ass sister, man? Do you think she will be happy to see me?" He said with an evil smirk on his face. Ever since we were kids, he always used to fuck with me by talking about my sister. He doesn't like her, he just knows that I hate when he flirts with her.

"Aye, yo' ass better fucking watching, my nigga, and I don't know if she would be happy to see you. Shit, you better hope her ass doesn't kill you."

"She ain't gone kill her true love."

"You better stop saying that shit before her husband kill yo' ass." When I said that, the smile he was wearing quickly faded.

"Her ass is in a relationship?"

"She passed a relationship, my nigga; she's married as of yesterday."

"Damn nigga, sis and Terran snuck off to get married yesterday?" Teddy asked, sounding shocked. I just smiled and shook my head yes.

"Yep, they dumb ass went to Vegas and didn't tell anybody, but I'm happy for them." My phone started ringing and I smiled seeing that it was Nikki FaceTiming me.

"What's up, baby?" When I saw her face, I knew she was going to be on bullshit because she was mugging the fuck out of me.

"Where the fuck are you at, Jamal McDaniel? Did you forget that my sister and mama was coming over here?"

"Oh shit! My bad, baby I did forget. I was too busy running

my mouth with Juice ass and lost track of time."

"Juice? When did y'all get coo again?"

"Like an hour ago, the shit that happened in the past was Gritt's fault," I explained.

"Should have known. Hey, black ass!" She shouted.

"What's up, scrub?" I laughed and told her that I was on my way.

"Let me get out of here before I get in trouble. I will see y'all niggas on Sunday." I got up and walked out the office feeling better than I did when I first got here. I'm glad that Juice and I got our shit together, now I had to get my head on straight, so I could deal with Nikki's mama and sister.

• •

"I am so sorry that I'm late, baby. Some shit went down, and I had to make sure that shit was straight before I left," I tried to explain to Nikki as soon as I walked in the door.

"It's okay, baby, Cyn already called and told me that you had an emergency. Just hurry up and change clothes, before I curse my sister and mama out." I laughed and kissed her lips before going upstairs and taking a quick shower. Deciding to dress comfortably, I slipped on a pair of sweats, and a plain white tee. I slipped on my slides and walked downstairs. As soon as her sister saw me, her eyes automatically darted down to my penis. I shook my head and sat next to Nikki, not even bothering to speak to her.

"How are you doing today, Mrs. Whitfield?" She looked me up and down before giving me a stank face.

"I'm doing good, but you don't think you could have put on some better-looking clothes before coming down here?"

"He can wear whatever he wants to wear, mama."

"I thought this was your house, Nicole?" Her sister said, putting her two cents in.

"This is my house, so what are you getting at?"

"How come he has a key to your house and is changing clothes upstairs?" Once again, I just shook my head and chuckled. Every time I'm around these people they act like they are so much better than Nikki and me. It was really starting to get on my last nerves.

"Is this why y'all came over here, to judge me? He has a key and a change of clothes here because he is my man. Is that okay with y'all?"

"We came over here so we can spend time with you, not him?" Her mama said, looking me up and down. I can tell that Nikki was about to go off because she started shaking her legs. I understand that she wants to go off on her mother and sister, but she still needs to respect them and kill them with kindness.

"Will you two please excuse us for a minute? Nikki, can I see you in the kitchen?" She took a deep breath and nodded her head while following me.

"I don't know how much longer I can take them, Jamal, and if my sister keeps looking at you, I'm going to beat her ass." I picked her up and sat her on the counter while sliding my hand up her skirt. When I slipped two fingers inside of her pussy, she took a deep breath and let out a soft moan.

"I need you to calm down, baby. You and I both know the only reason why they are being this extra is because I'm in there with you. I will stay in the kitchen while you visit with them to avoid any more problems, okay?" I worked my fingers in and out of her as I did the come here motion waiting for her to answer.

"Mmm shit, baby." Seeing that her ass was enjoying it, I quickly pulled my fingers out and placed them in my mouth. She quickly opened her eyes and shot me an evil glare.

"I was just about to cum," she whined.

"Did you hear anything that I just said?"

"Yes, I heard everything, but I couldn't respond because that shit was feeling so good."

"Okay, now go in there and spend time with your family, you can get some dick when they leave, okay?" She blew out a breath of frustration and hopped off the counter.

"Fine." She kissed my lips before walking out the kitchen. I pulled out my phone and dialed Cyn's number.

"Hello?" She answered on the fifth ring.

"Damn sis, were you sleep?"

"Yes, but I'm up now, what's up."

"Nikki's sister and mama are here."

"Oh lord, are they on bullshit?"

"You know they stay on bullshit, I had to come in the kitchen just to stop me from cursing their ass out," I said, which caused her to laugh.

"Well, you know how they are when it comes to our family. They act like they are perfect just because they had a little more money coming in than us, but we are from the same broke ass hood."

"That's the same exact thing I said, sis, but I'm not tripping off of them motherfuckers. All I know is if they keep treating my girl like shit, then I'm going to have to say something to them."

"Please let me do it, Jamal. You know I have been waiting a long time to curse her stanky pussy ass sister out." Ever since we were little kids, Cyn and Nikki's sister never got along. I think it's because Nikki has a stronger bond with Cyn than she do her own sister and that made her jealous.

"Yo' ass have been waiting for this day, huh? Oh, I didn't tell you that I caught her staring at my dick when I was walking down the stairs."

"Who Nikki?"

"Nah, her sister." I heard somebody clear their throat and saw Netty standing in the doorway.

"Speaking of the devil," I said loud enough so that Cyn could hear me.

"That bitch just walked in?"

"Mhmm."

"Am I on speaker?"

"Yep."

"Listen here, bitch, you got one more time to come at my brother and best friend, and I'm gone drag yo' sloppy ass, and you better keep yo' eyes off of his penis before I take them bitches out and make you eat 'em. Do you understand me?" I guess she had never heard Cyn talk like that before because once she was finished, her mouth shot opened and she looked like she was scared.

"I know you heard my sister talking to you. She asked you if you understood what she was saying," I said, instigating.

"Yes, I understand," she whispered.

"Good, now why the fuck are you in here?"

"I just wanted to let you know that Nikki said you could come out because we are about to leave."

"Ah-ight, Cyn. Let me call you right back." I hung up and sat my phone on the counter while walking back in the living room and sitting by Nikki.

"Are you going to come over for dinner, Nikki?" Her mother asked as she was walking out the door.

"Is Jamal allowed to come?" She asked, being petty. Her mama looked me up and down one more time then focused her attention back on Nikki.

"If that's the only way to get you to come over, then yes."

"Well, we will be there. Bye." Nikki got up and closed the door behind them.

"Yo' family is crazy." She shook her head and straddled my lap.

"I love them, but I just can't be around them for so long, especially if they keep fucking with you. If they can't accept the fact that you are my man, and you or your family is not going anywhere, then I don't want anything to do with them. I might have to beat my sister's ass one good time if she keeps staring at yo' dick like she wants to taste it." I couldn't do nothing but laugh at her ass 'cause she was being serious as fuck.

"You don't have to worry about me giving this dick away to anybody because it's all your, baby girl."

"Oh, is it now?" She asked, biting her lip and unbuckling my pants[WGE1].

"You know it is."

"Well, are you going to finish what you started in the kitchen?" I smirked and laid her sexy ass on the couch. I watched as she played with her pussy for a moment before I smacked her hand away and replaced it with my tongue.

"Mmmm shit, Jamal," she moaned. I gently sucked her clit in to my mouth as I flicked my tongue across it vigorously causing her to tremble. She grabbed my head, holding me hostage, trying to drown me in her sweet juices. When I felt her about to cum, I quickly stood up and slid inside of her warm, wet pussy.

"I will never get tired of being inside this pussy," I moaned, tilting my head back. I grabbed both of her legs and placed them in my forearms giving me more access to my favorite place.

"Oh God, this feels so fucking good! Shit!" She yelled out in pleasure. She opened her eyes and focused on me as she started matching my thrusts and fucking me back. The sensation of her pussy tightened around my dick had me ready to bust.

"I'm about to cum!" She screamed, shaking uncontrollably under me. I wrapped my hand around her neck and started beating her pussy up until we both came together.

"We gone have to get a new couch," she said, while trying to catch her breath.

"Says who? We gone clean this bitch off and act like nothing has never happened."

"That's nasty, baby." She looked at me and frowned.

"Oh, so you think Cyn and Terran get a new couch every time they mess it up?"

"I'm pretty sure they don't, but I'm not them."

"Well, you are going to be today, now bring yo' ass upstairs, so we can get in the shower and go to sleep." Within the next hour, we were both passed out on the bed. I guess good sex knocks you out after all.

• •

"Baby, yo' little friends are downstairs," Nikki said, trying to push me out the bed. I opened my eyes and just stared at her.

It felt like I literally just closed my eyes and now her ass is up here bothering me.

"Tell them niggas to go the fuck home; I'm trying to sleep." I placed my arms over my eyes hoping she would go away so I could go back to sleep, but I was wrong.

"Nigga, didn't nobody tell you to be up all fucking night playing the game. If you want them to leave, then you get up and tell them because I'm not going back downstairs, and you need to get up anyways since we have to go over your parents' house for dinner."

"Yo' ass better be lucky you my girl 'cause I would have pushed yo' silly ass out the fucking bed. Move so I can get up." I climbed out of bed so I could handle my hygiene. Once I was done, I slipped on my pajama pants and made my way downstairs.

"Damn nigga, it took yo' ass long enough to get down here," Terran complained.

"Shut yo' ass up, nigga, and why the fuck is y'all in my house so fucking early?"

"We came to talk about your cousin and Derrick."

"By all means, please make my day," I said in a sarcastic tone. I honestly didn't feel like hearing about them unless it to kill them, but that hasn't happened yet.

"Man, so I was chilling with Cyn when my mama pulled up to my house saying that one of my neighbors from my old condo called her saying that Derrick was in my house and came out with about three duffle bags. Which they thought it was strange because I literally haven't been there in a year," Terran said, sounding pissed off.

"What was in the duffle bags?" I asked.

"All the money I had in that bitch. Man, this nigga done stole my fucking money and probably gave it to Gritt's grimy ass."

"That's not it though, bro," Juice said.

"What else is there?" I asked, confused.

"He stole more money from Cyn," Teddy said. I don't

understand why this nigga keeps coming for Cyn like her ass is not dangerous.

"She's not good at hiding her money or something?" Juice asked.

"You know damn well Cyn is smart as fuck when it comes her money, man. Gritt just knows every place that she keeps her money. This nigga went to her car lot and stole everything from out of her office. You already know that we went by every place that him and Derrick be at, but we still couldn't find them, so you know what that means," Teddy explained.

"Them niggas went into hiding, but that dont mean nothing. I'm going to find them within the next twenty-four hours. Them niggas ain't about to get away with that bullshit. I know Cyn ass is probably hot as fuck right now."

"Her ass has been on ten since she found out, man. I have never seen her this mad before, had a nigga in the house scared as fuck, man," Terran said with a serious expression, causing us to break out laughing. I know that a lot of people say when I get mad it's like the world is about to end to because I'm never in a bad mood, but when Cyn gets mad, it's very dangerous. If you even look at her wrong, she might shoot yo' ass.

"I tried to warn yo' ass from the beginning about her not playing when it comes to her money or her family. You think Kash is worse? Nah, my nigga, you haven't seen Cyn when she is really mad. Her ass shows no mercy to anybody."

"Why are y'all down here talking about my best friend like she's just some crazy chick?" Nikki interrogated, while walking in the kitchen.

"Because her ass is crazy and you know it, but what I need you to do is go back upstairs for a minute." She stopped doing what she was doing and quickly looked up at me.

"Who are you talking to like that, my nigga?"

"I'm talking to yo' ass, my nigga, now play with me if you want to. We are talking about something and I just need you to go upstairs for a couple of seconds." She looked at me for a moment before stomping up the stairs like she was a little ass kid.

"You got her ass spoiled, man," Teddy pointed out as he shook his head.

"I'm supposed to have her spoiled, man, she's my girl, but back to this situation. After we leave my parents' house today, I'm going to slide by Gritt's house, so I can see if he was dumb enough to leave something behind. Terran, I want you to go with me." Terran looked up at me with a frown on his face.

"I was going to go over to Derrick's house and do the same thing."

"I'm going to let Juice and Teddy handle that. Not trying to be a dick, but you sometimes let you and Derrick's relationship cloud your judge of character when it comes to him."

"You don't think Gritt does the same thing to you? I mean, his ass has been playing you this whole time." I couldn't do nothing but nod my head and laugh because he has a valid point.

"You're right, but the only difference is he is trying to kill me and my family this time. Before it was just petty stealing and lying, but he has never taken it this far."

"Yea, I'll have to agree with Jamal on this one, man. Ever since we were corner boys, we never had to worry about Gritt coming after us. This shit literally just happened like what a couple of months ago when you started coming around," Teddy said.

"Well, maybe it's because he is jealous of me or some shit," Terran replied.

"I don't know, and I honestly don't give a fuck at this point. The only thing I give a fuck about it ending his life right about now."

"What about Derrick, bro?" Teddy asked.

"Are we going to take care of him as well?"

"If Gritt doesn't first," I simply said.

"Why do you think Gritt is going to kill him?"

"Because he doesn't like to share for a very long time. If he feels like somebody is trying to take from him or is in competition with him, he is going to kill them no matter who you are." Terran laughed.

"I can't believe that nigga is still living. His ass should have been dead by now as many people as he stole from."

"That's true, but when people find out that he is my cousin, they spared his life, but let's get back on track. So after we are done eating and talking to my parents', we are going to and do whatever we can to figure out where these niggas went. I don't care what you find, if you think it's significant to finding them, then bring it. I don't want these niggas to live another day." I was tired of Gritt thinking that we are going to keep letting shit go because we are blood, this nigga has crossed the line too many times, and it's time for him to go.

"Ah-ight man, well we wanted to just come by and let you know, so you won't be thinking that we are doing shit without yo' ass. We will see yo' happy ass in about three hours," Terran said, walking out the door. When I was alone, I had to say a silent prayer to myself that my sister don't kill this man. I'm pretty sure her ass can't wait to get her hands on Gritt either.

"Nikki, bring yo' ass down here!" I yelled from the bottom of the stairs.

"Why are you yelling like a mad, man?" She walked down the stairs with a smile on her face. That's another reason why I know that she is the one for me, because just like me, her ass is always in a good mood.

"I just needed to see your beautiful face before I lose my mind. What are you putting on today?"

"I don't know honestly. I was thinking about this crop top sweater that I got from Fashion Nova since it's going to be chilly outside, but I don't know yet. Why?"

"'Cause yo' ass like to show out and show too much skin. I'm honestly not feeling the whole crop top thing."

"Oh, negro please, I don't say nothing about you wearing gray sweat pants," I smirked because I knew she was going to say something about that. She hates when I wear sweat pants, but there is nothing that I could do about that. I can't help that God blessed a nigga with a long dick.

"Why would you be saying something about it anyways?"

"Don't play with me, Jamal. Every time you had gray sweat pants on, and we go somewhere, I have to curse these bitches out for looking at what's mine. I should go upstairs and cut them bitches up, huh?" She said with a mischievous grin on her face. I picked her ass up and sat her on the counter in the kitchen.

"Yo' ass plays way too much. I need you to try and talk to yo' best friend before we get to my mama's house because her ass is going to be on one."

"What happened? Did that pussy ass nigga Terran do something to her?" She was about to hop off the counter, but I quickly stopped her.

"Calm yo' ass down, Nikki. Terran did not do anything to her, Gritt stole more of her money from the car lot, and she's beyond pissed."

"Oh well, yea I will call her right now. I don't feel like dealing with a grumpy Cyn today." She hopped off the counter and went back upstairs. I grabbed a bottle of water from the fridge and chilled in the living room until it was time to go to my parents' house.

"What did Cyn say when you talked to her?" I asked Nikki as we both got out the car and made our way inside the house.

"That I can't tell her what to do because she is grown as fuck, and we need to leave her alone before she starts shooting everybody." I shook my head and walked in the kitchen where my mama was. It's gone take more than a talk with Nikki for Cyn to calm down.

"Hey, beautiful," I complimented my mother, kissing her cheek.

"Well, hello there, my handsome son. How are you today?"

"I'm better now that I'm looking at your wonderful face."

"Oh you're just laying it on thick today, aren't you? Move out my way, suck up." Nikki pushed me out the way and hugged my mama who just laughed.

"You two are crazy. How are you doing, Nikki?"

"I'm good, do you need some help in here?"

"You know I do, baby. Jamal go downstairs and play with your father while we get dinner ready. Has anybody talked to my daughter?"

"I talked to her this morning, but she's not in the best of mood today," Nikki replied.

"Oh lord, what done happened now?"

"You're about to be short a nephew," I simply said before walking out the kitchen and downstairs. I don't want to mess up the dinner by bringing Gritt up, but I feel like they should know that he's about to die before they find out by somebody else.

"What's going on, old man?" My pops looked up from the tv and smiled.

"What's going on, son?"

"Shit, I can't call it, what's been going on with you?"

"I should be asking you the same exact thing. You and your sister act like y'all can't call or stop by," he fussed.

"I know, pops. W e have just been so busy with some bull-shit lately."

"Yea okay, you just make sure that my baby is safe out there before I have to make an appearance." Although my pops had been telling Cyn and I our whole lives that he has never been in the streets or dealt with drugs, I think he is lying because there is no way that I just decided to start trapping on my own. Yeah, I started selling weed because it hurt to see my parents' struggling, but this shit didn't just come naturally it had to be in my blood.

"Cyn is not who you need to be worried about, trust me." Cyn and I vowed that we will always tell my parents what's going on even if it hurts them.

"What do you mean, son?"

"Gritt stole more money from her and now she's on a rampage. I know you haven't seen her in action before, but she knows how to handle herself well, pops." My pops couldn't do anything but shake his head at Gritt.

"What are y'all down here talking about?' Teddy asked. I

125

looked at saw Juice and Terran right behind him.

"Have y'all been together the whole fucking day?" I joked.

"Oh lord, I think he's getting jealous," Juice joked.

"Wait so, you and Teddy and okay with Juice now?" My pops asked with a smile on his face.

"Yea, Gritt was also the reason why we started beefing in the first place."

"Well, I'm glad that y'all are friends again. It's nice to see you, Joseph."

"Y'all come up here and eat!" My mama yelled from the top of the stairs. When we all made it in the dining room, I looked around and didn't see my sister.

"Where is my twin?" I asked.

"Upstairs in her old room. Maybe you can talk her in to coming down here," my mama said, sounding worried. I nodded my head and walked to the room. When I opened the door, Cyn was sitting by the window smoking a blunt.

"You know if mama finds out that you're smoking in here, she is going to beat yo' ass," I joked, while sitting on the bed.

"What the fuck is wrong with yo' cousin, Jamal? Why do he think that it's okay to do this shit to us?" She took another pull from the blunt and closed her eyes.

"Money and the wanting of power can change people, sis. We both knew how Gritt got down, but we never actually sat down and tried to help him, you know."

"Do you think he would have wanted our help? I mean, yea we should have talked to him about what he was doing, but we have always had his back no matter what the situation was. Not once did we give him a reason to turn on us, and why is he only targeting me and my husband?" Cyn was speaking facts, but I couldn't give her a good enough reason as to why he did the shit that he did.

"Well, we can ask him when we find him, but I just want to let you know that I am tired of giving him chance after chance. It's time that we kill him."

"Oh, letting him live was definitely out the question. This

is the second time that this nigga stole money from me and you know I needs my cash, so he has to die, but I think that since he is our blood, then we should be the ones to kill him."

"I think Money and Kash should kill Gritt and Derrick since they stole from them," I suggested.

"Are you sure that's what you want, bro?"

"Positive, I'm just ready to get this over with."

"I don't think that we really need to kill Derrick. I feel like if we just talk to him and tell that he needs to leave and give him money, then he will not be a problem. He just likes to act out when he gets really upset, but I don't think that he will cause any harm, because he still hasn't told anybody about Terran and I."

"Well, you're right about that, but it's all up to yo' man, sis. Now can we go downstairs because a nigga is hungry." She did not respond, because she was too busy looking out the window with a strange look on her face.

"Did you get a bitch pregnant and forget to tell us, Jamal?"

"What the fuck are you talking about?" When I walked over towards her, I saw a pregnant bitch walking up the driveway looking tired as shit.

"She looks familiar as fuck," I said.

"I know and I'm about to find out who she is right now." She grabbed the gun that she always have here and walked downstairs.

"You gone shoot a pregnant bitch, sis?" I asked, laughing.

"If she's on bullshit then hell yea I will."

"What's going on?" Terran asked with his gun at his waist. I just laughed and shook my head. These two crazy niggas are meant for each other.

"Can I help you?" Cyn asked. The girl looked at Cyn's gun and became nervous.

"Um, I'm looking for Terran or Money," she whispered. Cyn and I automatically looked at Terran with our guns aimed at him. If this nigga got another bitch pregnant, then he's a dead man walking.

CHAPTER 11

CYN

"Care to explain to me why this bitch came to my parents' house asking for you or Money?" I tilted my head to the side waiting for him to answer, but he looked like he was lost as fuck.

"Excuse..."

"If I was you I would just be quiet, little mama," Jamal said, laughing. His ass is pissing me off to because he always thinks shit is funny.

"You better chill the fuck out and get over here while you're smiling in her face," Nikki warned.

"I don't know this girl, Cyn. Damn," Terran yelled.

"So why is she coming here asking for you? I'm confused."

"I don't fucking know, Cynthia God damn! She's standing right in your face, ask her." To stop myself from killing his sarcastic ass, I turned around and just looked at her waiting for her to answer. When she got the hint, she opened her mouth and started talking.

"I'm Gregory... I mean, Gritt's baby mother and the reason why I know where your mother stay is because he had the address in his old phone." When she said something about being Gritt's baby mother, we all looked at each other with a confused expression.

"Gritt ain't never mention having a girlfriend so where did you really come from?"

"Cyn, move out the way and let that girl in. She already look like she been through it," my mama said about to get cursed out.

"Go back in the dining room and sit down, Mother Goose," Jamal said, causing everybody to laugh except for him.

"I didn't know anything that was going on until last night.

He said that he kept me a secret so he could protect me."

"So you didn't know about him stealing and setting us?" I asked.

"No, I didn't. I honestly didn't know that he was Gritt until last night. Everyone has been talking about him in the hood, but I did know it was him because I only know him as Gregory." I looked back at Terran, and he nodded at me letting me know that he believed her. I looked down and noticed that she didn't have any shoes on, and her clothes were all worn out.

"Did you walk here?" She cried and nodded her head yes. The attitude that I had instantly went away and I started feeling sorry for her.

"Why didn't you drive?" I asked.

"As soon as I found out who he really was, I left everything that he gave me at the house and just started walking because I didn't want y'all to think that I had anything to do with him stealing."

"You live far from here?" She cried harder and nodded her head yes.

"It's an hour drive just to get here. It took me four hours just to get here." I grabbed her hand and guided her upstairs to my bedroom.

"Just sit right here, and I'm going to get you some changing clothes, okay? I am so sorry about how I acted downstairs, it's just so much going on right now, and we just had to be sure that you weren't on any bullshit." She nodded her head and chuckled.

"It's okay, I totally understand, and I want to help you guys out with finding him. Even if it's to kill him. I don't want anything to do with him, and I want to make sure that he doesn't come after my baby. My name is Valencia, by the way."

"You don't worry about that right now. You can shower in here, everything you need will be in the closet. I will sit come clothes on the bed for you, and when you're done just come downstairs so you can eat something because I know you and my little cousin is hungry." I rubbed her stomach then walked downstairs. When I walked back in to the dining room, I sat down next to Terran and started eating off his plate like nothing ever happened.

"So what did she say?" He asked, while fixing him another plate.

"She didn't really say anything because I wanted her to get herself together first. She has already been through so much, and I didn't want to stress her or the baby out any more than she already is, but she did say that she wanted to help find him."

"Find him for what?" My mama asked.

"So we can kill him. He has been stealing and setting us up, mama. We have been giving him chances to clean up his act, but when he tried to turn Juice on us that crossed the line. Yo' nephew has been living foul and he needs to be taken care of." My mama looked at us before she started smiling.

"You father and I was trying to figure out how long it would take y'all to figure out that he has been against y'all this whole time."

"Wait... so y'all knew this whole fucking time and didn't think to tell us?" I yelled.

"First of all, you need to watch your mouth when you're talking to me. We knew when y'all were little kids, but we agreed to let y'all learn on y'all own that you can't always trust family."

"I told y'all they were some gangsters!" Jamal said, standing up and clapping.

"No, we are not gangsters, but our parents used to be, so that's where y'all get it from."

"Um, Cyn?" I turned around, and Valencia was standing in the doorway, looking ten times better. I quickly got up and walked over to her.

"What's up, love?"

"I'm all done, is there a place where I can throw my old clothes and the towel I was using?"

"Oh, I got it, baby. You just sit down and eat you something," my mama said, smiling and walking up the stairs.

"You can come sit next to me because you're getting too comfortable with my best friend," Nikki's jealous ass said. Valencia just laughed and sat down. Once I had her plate fixed, I sat it in front of her and poured her a glass of water.

"Baby, can I talk to you for a minute?" Terran whispered in my ear so I got up and nodded my head.

"Don't be bothering her while she eats either," I warned before walking in the guest bedroom with Terran.

"What's up, daddy?"

"I'm not trying to start shit, but I think Nikki and Gritt had something going on." I looked at him like he was crazy before bursting out laughing.

"Boy, I'm not about to play with you. Where did you get that from?"

"The way she was acting with Valencia. When she first came in and said that she was his baby mama, you should have seen her face, and what she just did when Valencia came back downstairs. Either she is real overprotective of this family, or she's been fucking Gritt and not telling anybody."

"You're tripping," I simply said. I don't think that Nikki would do something like that to Jamal, and if she would, then I'm just gone have to beat her ass.

"Okay, just make sure you watch her. Shit is getting crazy, and the last thing we need is be blind sighted and get caught slipping." I wrapped my arms around him and kissed his soft lips.

"I'm ready to go home, I'm not feeling good," I said, changing the subject.

"Okay let's go. Do you want Valencia to go with us just for safety?"

"Please." He nodded his head and followed back in the room.

"I think we are about to go home, since this dinner didn't go as planned. Valencia, do you know where you're staying?" She held her head down and shook her head no.

"I don't have a place to stay or no money."

"Well, you can come and stay with me and Terran over here."

"Are you sure? I don't want to be a burden."

"You're not a burden, love. We can take you by your old house so you can get some clothes and everything that you need."

"Oh shit, baby, I forgot I was supposed to ride with Jamal to Gritt's old place," Terran said.

"Go ahead, baby; we will be fine. Are you ready, Valencia?"

"Umm yes, but I don't want to get anything from the house because it doesn't belong to me."

"Oh girl, I'm pretty sure we all paid for that stuff in there, you will be okay. Nikki, do you want to go?" I asked to see what she was going to say.

"Nah, I'm good."

"Why don't you want to go?"

"Because I don't." I shook my head and started walking out the door.

"Okay, girl." When I got in the car, I pulled out my phone and texted Jamal.

Me: You need to watch Nikki 'cause T said that she has been acting weird ever since Valencia came along and I kind of see it.

Twin: Already on it. I would hate to have to handle her too.

ME: YOU AND ME BOTH, BROTHER

I slipped my phone in my pocket and drove off. Nikki has been my best friend since we were kids and if I find out that she is doing my brother dirty, I won't have a problem with putting a bullet in her.

• •

"Do you mind if I come in and look around?" I asked as we pulled up to her driveway.

"Sure, come on." I got out and followed her to the door. She stopped dead in her tracks and just looked around like she didn't recognize her own house.

"Are you okay, Valencia? What's wrong?" I asked getting worried.

"None of his things were here when I left last night. It looks completely different."

"Who the fuck are you and what are you doing here?" Some big black dude asked with his gun aimed at me. Valencia tensed up and started backing away.

"Here, take the keys and go wait in the car, okay." She was hesitant for a moment before nodded her head and quickly walking away. Once I noticed that she was safe in the car, I turned back around and just stared at the guy.

"Where is Gritt?" I asked, unfazed by him trying to scare me.

"Look, Cyn, I don't want to hurt you, but you have to get out of here before Gritt comes back."

"Do me a favor and don't let him know I was here, and if

you want to keep your life, then I suggest you don't be here tomorrow night. I want Gritt to be settled in before I end his life. Matter of fact, come take a ride with me so I can show Money who his new bodyguard is." He smiled happily and followed me outside. I pulled out my phone out and called T.

"What's up, baby?"

"Hey, can you have Money meet me at the warehouse like now?"

"You got something?"

"Mmmhmm," I simply said, looking in the rearview mirror at the guy.

"We will be there in five," he said then hung up the phone. I just smiled to myself and continued to drive. When we made it to the warehouse, everybody was already there.

"Stay in the car for me, okay?" Valencia smiled and nodded her head.

"Come on, big man so you can meet your new boss." He quickly got out the car and followed me.

"Yo Juice, can you go outside and sit with Valencia for me, please?"

"I got you, sis." When we walked in the warehouse, everybody was sitting down looking defeated.

"This better be good, baby 'cause we couldn't find shit. Gritt cleaned out his house and everything," Terran said, looking the dude up and down.

"I thought you said I was going to meet Money."

"You looking at him," Terran said with a devilish grin on his face.

"So if you're Money, then that means you must be Kash."

"Now that you solved the puzzle, can you tell me why he is here, baby?"

"Oh my bad, Money. He is Gritt's bodyguard that we are paying for with our money."

"Oh really? So that means that Gritt is still here, huh?"

"Yep, his dumb ass took over Valencia's house."

"And this was his bodyguard?"

"He pulled a gun out on me," I said acting like I was pouting. Terran grabbed his gun and put it in the dude's face.

"Like this, baby, or was it touching yo face like this?' He shoved the gun in his mouth and looked back at me waiting for me to answer.

"I don't really remember, but I think that's where it was," I said, while smiling.

"Do we need him for anything?" I shook my head no.

"Good 'cause my trigger finger has been itching for a minute." Without any hesitation, he pulled the trigger splattering blood everywhere.

"Damn, can you warn a nigga next time?" Teddy complained, while taking his shirt off.

"My bad, nigga, but the sight of blood just excited me. So when are we planning on killing Gritt?" I picked up a wet towel and wiped his face off.

"Tomorrow night. He's paranoid as fuck right now, so I want to give him some time to get comfortable enough to let his guard down then Kash and Money will be personally killing his ass since he stole from us. Anyways, I got Valencia in the car, and I need to get her home so she can get comfortable. I will see you at the house." I kissed his lips and walked out the door. Once I was outside, I saw Juice leaning on the car on his phone.

"Why standing out here in the cold instead of sitting in the warm car?"

"That bitch is crazy," he complained.

"What do you mean she's crazy?"

"She kicked me out the car because I was trying to smoke." I shook my head and laughed.

"Well, she is pregnant, idiot."

"What does her being pregnant have to do with anything? My mama smoked weed when she was pregnant with me and looked how I turned out."

"I'm not even gone justify that with a response. Get off my car, so I can get out of here crazy." He gave me a hug then walked back in the warehouse.

"Ready to go home?"

"Yes, but is this what you and your family have to deal with every day?" I shook my head no and laughed.

"Girl, no, this shit just started happening like two months ago when yo' man lost his mind."

"I can't believe that I didn't see anything of this going on before now."

"Oh, girl, yo' man was good at hiding shit. It took Jamal and I a long ass time to figure that out. Just be glad you got away before he was able to turn on you." I could tell that she was stuck in her thoughts because she stopped talking and just stared out the window. We stopped at some store so she could get some things for her and the baby since she is going to be here in three months.

"Thank you so much for everything, I really appreciate it," she said, while helping me with the bags.

"You don't have to thank me, girl. I did this because I wanted to."

"Can I ask you a question?"

"What's on yo' mind, sweetheart?"

"Why don't yo' best friend like me? I feel like she was being very childish, and she doesn't even know me." I knew something had to be off for Valencia to notice it. Nikki has never acted like this with anybody before, so I'm just trying to figure out what's going on with her.

"I honestly don't know what her problem is, but I definitely noticed something weird about her today. If you want, I can talk to her about it?"

"Okay, because I don't want to start problems with anybody."

"Don't worry about Nikki and her attitude problems, girl. You need to be focused on that little girl in your stomach."

"I'm so excited to meet my baby girl! I feel like once she's here, then I will be complete." Seeing how happy she was as she talked about her child made me feel like I wanted a child.

"Do you know what you're naming her?" I asked.

"Gabriella. Do you want kids?"

"I don't know honestly."

"What do you mean?" I asked curiously.

"Before I got married and met you, I never really thought about having kids, but now I want to know what it feels like to be pregnant and to have a baby."

"Are you pregnant now?" She caught me off guard with that question. Her ass had me shook.

"No, why would you ask that? Do I look pregnant?"

"Who's pregnant?" Terran asked with a serious look on his face.

"You are so nosey, aren't you? Valencia, your room is going to be the first door on the left. Nobody has ever been in there, so the sheets are clean, there is also a tv and laptop in the room just in case you need some entertainment." She stood up and hugged me tightly.

"Thank you soo much! I promise I will be out of here before my daughter is born, and I will be looking for a job while I'm here."

"You don't need to be working and you're about to give birth. Let me see what I can do, and we are not rushing you to leave." She hugged me one more time then walked away with Terran behind her carrying her bags. I pulled out my phone and text Nikki.

ME: ARE YOU BUSY?

Nikki: No. What's up, love?

ME: DO YOU THINK YOU CAN COME OVER SO WE CAN TALK?

NIKKI: OMW

"Who are you texting that has yo' face all balled up?" Terran asked, scaring me. He wrapped his arms around me and walked me to the couch.

"Nikki. I really hope she is not on any funny shit, Terran 'cause I would really hate to kill my best friend." He pulled me on his chest and sighed.

"I hope not either, but the way she was acting today was kinda of weird."

"I love her to death, but I don't have a problem with killing my best friend."

"When are you going to talk to her about it?"

"She's supposed to be coming over here today so we can talk about it. Do you really think she would do something like that to me?" I know I said that I don't have a problem with killing my best friend, but I really don't even want to think about having to do anything like that to Nikki. I just hope and pray that this is a big misunderstanding of some sort.

"Well, I hope she doesn't say or do anything that is going to piss you off because the last thing we need is a pissed off, Cyn," he said, which caused the both of us to laugh.

"You're right because I tend to lose my mind when I'm pissed."

"What were you and Valencia talking about before I walked in the house." He asked, changing the subject.

"What are you talking about?" I said, trying to play stupid.

"Act dumb if you want to, I know what I heard when I was walking in."

"She asked me if I wanted a baby, Terran."

"And what did you say?"

"I told her that I did, but at the same time I didn't."

"Why not though?"

"I guess I never really thought about it like that. I mean, now that I'm married, I do want to give you some babies, but before then I never really wanted babies. I don't have a particular reason as to why, I just don't. Do you want kids?" I explained, shrugging my shoulders.

"I want a whole bunch of kids running around here getting on our nerves. I want to keep my legacy alive." I couldn't help but smile as his face lit up when he started talking about wanting kids. I never really thought about how having kids would make him feel.

"I do think that I should take a pregnancy test." His face lit up as soon as I said that.

"You think we're pregnant?"

"No I don't, but Valencia said that I was glowing and I might be pregnant. I don't believe her, but I do just want to make sure before I start doing irresponsible things."

"Knock knock." Terran and I both stopped talking and focused our attention on Nikki, who walked in with a smile on her face like she didn't just have an attitude a couple of hours ago. Terran got up and chuckled.

"I'm about to go to the store to get what you wanted. I need her gone and you in the bed butt ass naked when I get back." He kissed me then slapped my ass before walking out the door. Nikki smiled and sat down in front of me.

"So what's on yo', mind Cyn?" I closed my eyes and told myself to calm down.

"I'm going to get straight to the point because I don't want to beat around the bush. Are you and Gritt fucking?" The smile she was wearing quickly faded and changed to anger.

"Why the fuck would you ask me some dumb ass shit like that, Cyn? Why in the fuck would you think that I'm fucking Gritt when I'm with Jamal and that nigga ain't shit?"

"First of all, I'm going to need you to bring your voice

down a couple of notches before I beat yo' ass, and the reason why I asked you is because it was brought to my attention by Jamal and Terran."

"Why would they think that though?"

"Because yo' ass has been acting weird ever since Valencia came here. That girl doesn't even know you, but you sure was mugging her like she ate yo' cooking or something." She looked at me and started laughing.

"I wasn't mugging her because of Gritt's ass; I was mugging her because you have been all up on her ever since she came wobbling her ass on yo' mama's porch. I would never stoop that low and start fucking with Gritt, and it's fuck up that you think I would even do something that foul to you or Jamal." I could tell that she was really hurt, but I honestly could care less at the moment.

"So you was mad at Valencia because you don't want me to be paying attention to her?"

"Yep."

"That some kid shit, Nikki. That girl walked three hours to my home in some worn out shoes, and dingy clothes all because of some shit that my cousin did, and on top of that, I pulled a gun out on the girl, so excuse me for trying to be a good person."

"Bitch, when are you ever a good person? You have been a bitch ever since we were little, so you can try again with that lame ass excuse." I snickered and started scratching my head.

"I don't know what your problem is, but I need you to chill the fuck out with that sarcastic shit 'cause everything I said was the truth. Now is not the time for you to be getting smart and shit 'cause I will shoot yo' ass and not think twice about it." I guess she realized that I was serious because she looked at me then took a deep breath.

"So you're not trying to replace me with her?"

"Are you being serious right now, Nikki?"

"Yes, I'm being serious, Cynthia. When you and Terran first got together, I barely saw you, and I was jealous because I didn't have you to myself anymore. Now that Valencia is here and staying with you, not only do I have to share you with Terran, now I have to share you with that bitch and I'm not feeling that," she whined. I forgot how spoiled Nikki was, so I guess I understood where she was coming from because I would honestly feel the exact same way, but I wouldn't let her ass know that.

"You don't have to worry about me replacing you with anybody because you already know that I don't like bitches that much to be hanging out with them, and because I don't have time to be making friends. The next time you are feeling some type of way about anything, I'm going to need you to say something instead of being rude to somebody who you don't know. She is a very sweet and innocent girl."

"I know. I'm so sorry for acting crazy, are we okay?"

"Yea, we are okay, but what you need to do is go home and try to explain to your man why you was acting crazy because he's thinking the same thing that Terran is thinking." She grabbed her things and stood up.

"I will call you when I get home." She kissed my cheek and walked away. Once she was gone, I let out a sigh of relief that I didn't have to kill my best friend because I would've been crushed. The only thing that I had to worry about now was being pregnant, and that's something that I don't know if I'm ready for.

CHAPTER 12

TERRAN

"Damn baby, what's taking so fucking long?" I asked for the millionth time, probably about to get cursed out. I was currently standing outside of our bathroom waiting for her to come out and tell me if we are about to have a baby or not.

"If you ask me that one more god damn time, I'm going to piss on you, my nigga." She walked out the bathroom with a mug on her face, which had me cracking up.

"What the fuck is funny?"

"Yo ass is being real extra. I told you that it takes five minutes for the results to be accurate and you keep asking me the same fucking question over and over again like that is going to make it go faster."

"My bad, baby, I'm just excited about the thought of you being pregnant." I pulled her towards me and kissed her lips. She looked at me with a serious expression.

"You're not scared of being a parent?"

"Hell no I'm not. Why would be, baby?"

"I mean, I'm not scared to be a parent technically, I just don't want our babies to grow up barely making it like me and my brother did. I guess I just want to give them what I didn't have when I was growing up. I have amazing parents, but it just hurts to see them struggling."

"Well, that's one thing that you don't have to worry about because we are going to be smart and responsible when it comes to finances. We are going to start saving money every chance we get so they don't have to worry about anything."

"I love you so much, baby. Do you know that?" She asked, while looking me in the eyes.

"Isn't that why you married me?"

"Nope, I married you for the money," she said with a smirk on her face.

"Keep playing with me if you want to and yo' ass is going to be divorced." She laughed and walked away while waving her ring in the air.

"Let me go see if you're going to be my baby daddy so I can go ahead and put you on child support."

"Keep playing with me if you want to, and I'm going to be a single father," I joked, while walking back and forth. I have never been this nervous about anything a day in my life. If Cyn is pregnant that would make me the happiest man alive.

"Baby, I got some bad news." When she came out looking sad, I felt like my world was taken from me. The thought of having a baby of my own was like music to my ears, but I guess it wasn't our time yet.

"It's okay, baby, we can try again," I said, but she looked at me like I said something wrong.

"That's not why I'm sad. I'm mad that I'm going to be stuck with yo' big head ass for the next eighteen years," she replied, pulling the pregnancy test out of her pocket and handing it to me.

"Are you being serious right now, baby?" She smiled and nodded her head yes. I happily picked her up and kissed her passionately.

"Yes, I am, daddy."

"You just made me the happiest nigga alive, ma. Thank you so much for giving me my first child. I love you so much."

"I love you too, baby. Do you think we can go to the doctor tomorrow just so they can see how far along I am?"

"Yea we can do that. I need to stop by my mama's house after so I can tell her about us being married and having a baby." My mama is going to be happy about Cyn being pregnant, but I don't know how she is going to feel about us getting married and not telling her.

"Now that I'm thinking about it, I haven't even told my parents that we're married. We are going to get killed twice,"

Cyn said, shaking her head.

"Well, we have to get it taken care of tomorrow before we have to deal with Gritt and Derrick."

"I'm ready to get this over with. Oh and Nikki is not fucking Gritt," she said, while stripping out of her clothes and getting in the bed.

"Are you sure she's not?"

"Positive, she said the reason why she was acting like that is because she was jealous basically." I stripped down to my boxers and got in bed right after Cyn.

"What is up with everybody getting jealous of shit that we can't control?" I complained.

"I mean, I can kind of understand why Nikki was jealous. Before you came along, we literally stayed with each other every single day, then when I got in a relationship, she had to share me which was a hard thing to do. Now that Valencia is here and she saw how fast her and I clicked, she started to think that I was going to replace her, so that's what made her not like Valencia," Cyn tried to explain.

"That's childish as fuck."

"Same thing I said, but I'm just glad that she wasn't on no bullshit."

'Yea me too because she's really coo." When Cyn didn't respond, I looked down at her and noticed that her ass was knocked out. I swear this girl could go to sleep fast as fuck. I kissed her lips and drifted off to sleep thirty minutes later.

• •

"Baby, will you be still? I told you that everything is going to be okay." We were at the doctor's office waiting to see someone.

"You don't know if it's going to be okay or not, jackass. I told you that I was smoking weed yesterday."

"Okay, and what's wrong with that?"

"Nothing is wrong with it; I just don't want anything to affect my baby that's all."

"I'm going to need you to calm the fuck down and stop

worrying about shit that you don't need to worry about. Out baby is going to be fine."

"How are you guys doing today?" The doctor said, walking in with the equipment that he needed. Instead of responding, Cyn just smiled and looked away.

"Excuse her, she's just nervous, but we are doing good, just ready to see what's going on."

"Well, let's get started, shall we." He put the gel on Cyn's stomach and got to work. When I looked at the screen, I didn't even know what in the fuck I was looking at.

"Is that my baby?" Cyn asked in awe.

"Yes ma'am, but you are actually having twins. Here is baby number one, and here is baby number two." Cyn and I just sat there staring at each other with big ass smiles on our face. If she thought I was going to act crazy with one child, then she better get ready because I'm about to be real protective over my babies.

"Do you know how far along I am?" Cyn asked, swiping away the tears.

"It looks like you're about twelve weeks old." I looked at Cyn, confused.

"That's approximately three months, baby," she said, laughing at me.

"Well shit, I don't know what none of that shit means. Are my babies doing well?"

"Everything looks good to me. Make sure you call within the next couple of days to schedule an appointment." He grabbed some tissue and was about to wipe that shit off, but I stopped him.

"Aye, my nigga, don't be trying to feel on my wife and shit. I'll wipe that shit off, and you can get the fuck out." I snatched the tissue out his hand and wiped my wife's stomach.

"I'm so sorry about his attitude, he has an overprotective problem when it comes to me." Cyn tried to explain to the doctor before slapping my arm. The doctor didn't say anything else, he just gathered his things and walked out the door.

"I hope you don't get mad, but I already got the names picked out, and they are unisex names," I mentioned which made her blush.

"I'm not mad, baby. Actually I'm kind of glad that you picked out the names because I'm bad at it. What are they?"

"Santana and Montana."

"I LOVE THAT!" She screamed excitedly while clapping her hands together.

"I'm glad you do because I wasn't going to change it if you didn't." She mugged me and grabbed my hand while we walked out the door.

"So are we going to your mom's house first or do you think we should go by my parents' house?"

"Shit it doesn't matter to me, baby. We are going to get cursed out at both so we might as well just go to your parents' house first." I opened the door to help her in the car.

"Let me call Jamal and see where he is at." When she pulled out her phone and dialed his number, it went straight to voicemail, which was weird because he never lets his phone go under fifty percent.

"Let me call Nikki." I nodded my head and pulled out the hospital's parking lot.

"Cyn, please don't be mad at me," Nikki said with a shaky voice as soon as she answered the phone.

"Where is my brother at, Nikki?"

"Cyn..."

"Nikki, where is my brother at and why is his phone going straight to voicemail?" She asked in a calm manner.

"The hospital." I busted a U-Turn in the middle of the street and made my way to Nikki's house.

"Why?" I ain't gone lie and say that it wasn't scaring me to see Cyn this calm because it was, but it was also turning me on.

"Because I shot him, but he was going to kill me if I didn't shoot Jamal."

"Who was?"

"Juice." Cyn looked at me and chuckled.

"Can you call Juice for me?" I nodded my head yes and pulled over. I pulled out my phone and dialed his number.

"What's up, bro?" He answered on the first ring.

"What are you up to, my nigga?"

"Shit, over here chilling with Teddy, what's going on? Y'all good?"

"Jamal is in the hospital and I was just told that it was by you."

"WHAT THE FUCK DO YOU MEAN IT WAS BY ME? Is he okay?"

"I don't know if he is okay or not, but we will meet you and Teddy at the hospital," I said then hung up the phone. When I looked at Cyn, I could tell that she blacked out because her eyes were ice cold.

"That bitch hung up as soon as she heard Juice's voice, and don't even bother going over there because I know for a fact that she's gone. Just go to the hospital so I can make sure my brother is good."

"What are you going to do about, Nikki?"

"I will personally handle her, but my main focus right now is Gritt. Can you call somebody so they can go and sit with Valencia just in case Nikki is on bullshit?"

"I got you, baby. I will shoot my mama a text."

ME: CAN YOU GO TO MY HOUSE AND WATCH THIS PREGNANT GIRL FOR ME?

Ma Duke: You better not have gotten a bitch pregnant that's not my daughter in law.

Me: Lol. No, ma she's a friend of Cyn.

Ma Duke: I got you, son. Call me and let me know if you're good.

"Mama is going over there." Cyn just nodded her head and looked out the window. I don't know what type of time Nikki is on, but if she was smart, she would be on the first flight out of here because Cyn is going to paint Compton red until she finds her.

"Excuse me, I'm looking for Jamal McDaniel's room," Cyn said nicely. The nurse looked at her then popped her gum.

"Can you have a seat and I will be right back with you please?" Cyn laughed and slapped the fuck out of that nurse.

"Listen here, little bitch. I'm not in a very good mood, and if you love your life, I suggest you get to typing on your computer and find out what room my brother is in."

"Cyn!" We heard Teddy and Juice yelled. Cyn punched the nurse one more time before walking away. Once she was close enough to Juice, she grabbed him by his jacket and pushed him in to the wall.

"Did you have anything to do with this?" She asked, getting straight to the point.

"I was with Teddy the whole fucking time, sis, and I will never do no bullshit like this."

"He's telling the truth, Cyn. We called Jamal like an hour ago to see if he wanted to come and smoke with us, but he was arguing with Nikki and said that he was going to call us back. He's in room 200 if you don't believe us." Instead of responding, we both just walked away and in to his room. I was glad to see that Jamal was sitting up, but he sure in the fuck was mad.

"It took y'all a long fucking time to figure out that I was damn near dead," he complained, being dramatic.

"We were at the hospital, what happened to you? Are you okay?" Cyn asked.

"This hospital?"

"Yes, I'm pregnant, so we had to come and just make sure that my babies were okay."

"Wait... pregnant? BABIES!" He said with a huge ass smile on his face.

"Jamal, focus. Who did this to you, and where were you shot at?"

"That bitch Nikki and her nigga shot me in my fucking arm. I can't stand bitches who don't have no aim." I looked at Cyn and started shaking my head.

"I told you that bitch was fucking, Gritt," I said.

"Nah, she ain't fucking Gritt, she's fucking Derrick."

"What!" Cyn and I both said at the same time. He just laughed and shook his head.

"Yep, I caught her on the phone with that nigga earlier, and I guess he heard us arguing, so he came to my house and told her if she doesn't kill me then he is going to leave her."

"And she shot you?" I smirked and nodded his head yeah.

"The only bitch who I wanted to be with turned out to be a fucking rat. Can you believe that shit? Oh but best believe I got a bullet with her name on it and I know for a fact that I won't miss." Derrick ass has to be on some type of drugs or something, because that type of shit is not in his blood.

"I'll take care of Derrick, bro. You just need to worry about your bitch."

"Nah, I got the both of them. You two just need to worry about finding and killing Gritt. I don't plan on being here for a long time. Plus I don't think that they will be a problem."

"Are you sure, bro?"

"Yea I'm sure, and if I need any help, then I will bring Teddy and Juice for a minute."

"Speaking of Juice, his ass was about to die in the lobby," I said, looking at Cyn.

"Why?"

"Because Nikki told yo' sister that Juice said that if she didn't shoot you, then he was going to kill her. Cyn's hulk ass literally picked him up and put him against the wall. I was in there dying on the inside." Jamal looked at Cyn and laughed.

"Yo' ass is crazy, but you can't be doing all that and you're pregnant."

"Negro please, I do whatever I want. We are about to get out of here so we can go and take care of Gritt. I don't care about whatever you're saying; I am going to help you find Nikki so I can personally kill that bitch because she sat there and lied to my face and my dumb ass believed it." I can tell that Cyn was more hurt than mad because she couldn't even look at nobody.

"I understand, sis. You just focus on Gritt, and getting all of your money that he didn't spend." He smirked.

"Haha, I will be back up here when I'm done. I love you." She bent down and kissed his cheek before walking out.

"Aye, bro, I know that my sister probably don't need to be watched, but just make sure that she is good 'cause she tends to get out of hand."

"I got you, bro. You know that I'm not going to let her do anything stupid, especially since she is pregnant with my babies."

"I know, bro. Both of y'all just be careful." We slapped hands and I walked out the room and met Cyn.

"You ready to go get this shit over with, baby?" She walked over to me and kissed my lips.

"Yea I'm ready. We need to go home so we can change clothes, I'm getting hyped just thinking about killing him." I shook my head and laughed.

"Well, let's do this shit, Kash." We walked out the hospital hand in hand, preparing for this massacre.

• •

"You ready to do this, bae?" Kash pulled her mask over her face and nodded her head. Not being able to resist, I pulled her towards me and kissed her lips. There is nothing sexier than seeing my wife taking the life of a nigga who crossed us.

"Let's do this shit then." We both cocked our guns and broke in the back door. The eerie feeling of being watched came over me which instantly made me watch my surroundings. This is not the first time my wife and I had to handle our own business because my team wasn't able to, but every now and then we had to get our hands dirty. I felt around the wall to figure out where the light switch was since we were literally standing in darkness, and the first thing that I saw were two bitches standing in front of me with a shotgun.

"These bitches think they're tuff, huh daddy?" Kash mocked, while handing me her gun.

"Who are you and what are you doing in this house?" One of them asked, trying to sound hard but was scared shitless.

"I don't like having conversations, little girl. Where is Gritt's grimy ass at?" I asked, while walking closer to them.

"You got five seconds to get out of here before the both of you lose y'all life." Kash looked at me then burst out laughing.

"They thought that little threat was going to work on us, baby. You see, I was going to let y'all bitches live, but since both of you are talking out the side of y'all neck, I have to kill y'all." She handed me her gun and walked towards both of them, not caring that they had guns in their hands. In one quick motion, Kash grabbed both of them and snapped their necks at the same time, making my dick hard.

"Damn baby, it turns me on when you get all gangsta on me," I whispered in her ear, while slapping her ass.

"Let's just get this over with so I can show you how gangsta I really am." She winked and walked out the kitchen. I stood there for a minute adjusting myself before following behind her. Walking through this house and looking at all the shit that Kash and I basically paid for pissed me off even more. When we made it to Gritt's room, we could tell he was in there because the smell of fear invaded my nostrils. We walked into the cold, dark room and just sat on the bed.

"Gritt, you might as well come out because we ain't leaving no time soon, buddy. My wife and I got all night, ain't that right, baby?"

"Nah, I don't have all night to be waiting on him. I'm trying to get home and fuck yo' brains out, so he might want to come out before I pay a visit to his pregnant girlfriend and make her take a nasty fall." Kash evil ass said with a smirk on her face. The mentioning of his girlfriend getting hurt triggered something inside of him because he automatically ran out the closet.

"Okay! Okay, here I am, please don't hurt my girlfriend."

"How are you doing, Gritt?" I asked, ignoring his last statement.

"Who are you guys?"

"Who we are has nothing to do with why we are here. Why have you been stealing from us, Gregory?" Kash asked, while filing her fingernails.

"Money and Kash?" The look on his face caused me to burst out laughing.

"Answer my wife's question, man."

"I always put back what I take. Please don't kill me."

"What do you mean you always put back what you take, Gritt? You stole a lot of money from me, my nigga. I've had yo' back since we were kids and you still fucked my brother and I over."

"What do you mean you and your brother? I don't even know who y'all are?" Gritt said with a confused look on his face. Kash looked at me and nodded her head. At the same exact time, we took our masks off revealing who we really are. Gritt looked for a moment before his hands flew over his mouth.

"Wait... so y'all are Kash and Money?"

"In the flesh," Kash said, laughing.

"Cyn and Terran?" As soon as he said our names, we both emptied our clips inside of him leaving him slumped over. Cyn was about to walk over to me, but she stopped dead in her traps when she saw me pull my gun off my waist. She quickly pulled her out and started looking around.

"Is somebody still in here, daddy?"

"Yea, just my competition who I have to get rid of." She tilted her head to the side confused about what I just said.

"Who is your competition?"

"You, and your brother. Oh, did you really think that I was going to be dumb enough to team up with some niggas who are on the same level as me and think I'm about to share my business? Nah, baby girl. The only reason why I got close to y'all, was so I can take over y'all business. Marrying you was all apart over the game, you just have to learn how to play it," I said, aiming my gun at her. She stood there for a minute before cocking her gun and aiming it at my head.

"Well, let the games begin baby...

TO BE CONTINUED...

[WGE1]You said he had on sweatpants

CPSIA information can be obtained
at www.ICGtesting.com
Printed in the USA
LVHW031727241220
675096LV00004B/458